GW01605354

The Continuing Adventures of Captain Gregory Dangerfield

The Continuing Adventures of Captain Gregory Dangerfield

JEREMY LLOYD

CASSELL
LONDON

This book is for the lovely Dale . . .
and a lucky young man called J.H.D.

CASSELL LTD.
35 Red Lion Square, London WC1R 4SG
and at Sydney, Auckland, Toronto, Johannesburg,
an affiliate of
Macmillan Publishing Co., Inc.,
New York.

First published 1979

ISBN 0 304 30308 9

Typeset by Inforum Ltd., Portsmouth.
Printed and bound in Great Britain by
Lowe & Brydone (Printers) Ltd.,
Thetford, Norfolk.

One

"And so Captain Gregory Dangerfield," said the tense voice of the late P. W. Arnold, "struggled valiantly for his life as the evil-smelling swamp sucked his brave body down to its doom. Was this the last time his clear blue eyes would see the sun that hung like a hot orange over the Javanese jungle; was this farewell forever to the bravest man in the world who was about to be sucked out of sight with a sardonic smile on his lips at the fickleness of fate?"

The keys of the ancient Imperial typewriter rattled away relentlessly on the marble washstand in the small upstairs room of 69 Ranleigh Road, Streatham, a room rented by Mr Henry Wordsworth Potts, a thin, pale-faced, youngish man with distraught hair, wearing an outsized Fair Isle pullover and a deep frown of concentration as he peers unseeingly ahead through his thick spectacles. Not at the keys on which his fingers leap up and down with such expertise, but apparently at his reflection in the washstand mirror. Two pairs of unseeing eyes gaze at each other. It is clear that the owner of the busy fingers is in a state of deep concentration, for, unknown to the outside world, at this very moment, Mr Henry W. Potts is once again in spiritual contact with the former tenant of his room, the late Mr P. W. Arnold. P. W. Arnold, creator of that handsome adventurer Captain Gregory Dangerfield, through the medium of his last treasured possession — the ancient Imperial typewriter — is communicating yet another of Dangerfield's breathtaking adventures to Mr Potts. Mr Potts is not only typing it, but from his tense expression it is clear that he once again became the late author's hero, lost somewhere in the 1920s in his reckless search for adventure.

A sardonic smile flickered over his lips as the keys rattled relentlessly on. Then, as the full implication of his plight struck him, it disappeared and his eyes took on an anxious look. He was looking at the seemingly harmless green carpet just under his nose, a carpet on which he had unwittingly placed his immaculately polished riding boot by Mirello of Milan only a few moments earlier. The boot now, together with its companion, was searching hopefully for terra firma.

As the toes of his expensive boots continued their fruitless search Mr Potts opened his mouth and taking a deep breath did something quite unusual for Dangerfield — he shouted "Help, P. W.". But apart from the croak of frogs, the squawk of some unseen jungle bird and the incessant hum of the gnats round his head that were having a quick snack before their lunch disappeared, the Javanese jungle was as silent as the grave that was slowly engulfing him.

As a bubble of evil smelling gas popped unpleasantly under his nose he wondered how Dangerfield was going to escape yet again from a seemingly hopeless situation and, as always, when all seemed lost the voice of Gregory Dangerfield's creator, the late P. W. Arnold, came to his rescue.

"Suddenly," it said, "Dangerfield's ears, said to be more sensitive than those of the fruit eating giant-eared Bombay bat, heard a twig break." Mr Potts strained his Bombay bat ears attentively. Yes, they definitely heard something, "followed," said the late P. W. Arnold, "by the sound of a voice — the gallant Captain recognised from long ago."

"Umbala, chook chook," said a high pitched voice nearby, and as Mr Potts peered hopefully over his spectacles at the bank, the bushes parted to reveal a beautiful girl dressed in a brief leopard skin. Despite her untidy hair and the bone through her nose, Mr Potts recognised her instantly as Miss Vera Jenkins from the Arthur Murray School of Dancing, whose premises, over Safeways in Streatham, he had recently been attending to learn the foxtrot, tango and free-style quickstep.

"It was," explained P. W. Arnold, "Princess N'Kooma, Jungle Goddess of the Frog People, whose life Dangerfield had saved some years before from the wrath of Ka the crocodile god, with whom he had fought an underwater duel to the death in the raging waters of the Racumba Falls, over which he had plunged still applying the crosslegged neck lock in the manner taught to him by Bandy Dan Barnaby the famous Cornish wrestler and cello player."

Mr Potts hoped that the story of his previous meeting with the Goddess of the Frog People was not going to be too lengthy as there was now little more than his nose, toupee and one arm protruding from his hungry grave. "And now," continued the Voice, "having seen the gallant Captain's balloon descend into the impenetrable jungle, she had swung through the trees with her faithful companion Umbala to investigate."

"Please help me," said Mr Potts, speaking slowly in case Princess N'Kooma's command of English was as limited as her appearance suggested. "By the Great Toad of the Temple of the Tree Frogs, is it you?" she gasped. "Is it Greg-ree, the Great White God from the clouds, who came in an iron bird many moons ago and saved me from the wrath of the god Ka?"

"Yes, it's me again," confirmed Mr Potts, nodding, then sticking up his nose like a periscope thinking what a pity it was that she spoke English at all and pointing to his fast disappearing head with his free hand he indicated urgently, that any further exchange could well be terminated rather abruptly.

Throwing her head back, Princess N'Kooma emitted a weird cry, "Aeeergh Umbaaala." Probably, thought Mr Potts, sadly, a native word that means "Goodbye White god," and as he prepared to join his creator on the other side of the grave he heard a crashing noise in the undergrowth. The bushes parted and an enormous gorilla, wearing a loin cloth, appeared. He was beating his huge fists on his chest, which sounded like a giant drum. He opened his mouth and let out the same cry that the Princess had used. Mr Potts instantly recognised Guy, the gorilla from Regent's Park Zoo, and hoped he'd not remember the rotten banana that Mr Potts had thrown to him last summer.

"Yes, this was Umbala, the missing link," said the voice of

the late P. W. Arnold, "her companion since he fell out of a tree as a baby." I shan't be here to hear how he cut his first tooth, thought Mr Potts as he closed his mouth tightly to stop the swamp coming in.

"Umbala, Na boo boo," said the Princess pulling a length of jungle vine into view. "Na gumba agu," she said pointing at Mr Potts' head. "She is," explained P. W. Arnold, "telling Umbala that he must save her friend." Mr Potts gazed at the narrow gap between Umbala's eyes and the top of his head and wondered whether there was room for all the information he had just received.

At that moment Miss Jenkins, who for the purpose of P. W. Arnold's story was now Goddess of the Frog People, threw the liana to Mr Potts, who caught it with his free hand and held on desperately as Princess N'Kooma wrapped the other end round Umbala's neck and uttered the life saving words "Na, gargoonooni."

As the massive Umbala gripped the vine in his vast hands and stepped back, the body of Mr Henry Wordsworth Potts inched out of the clinging mud, like a slowly drawn cork, freeing his other arm with which he grasped the vine.

"Dangerfield's giant muscles," said the approving voice of P. W. Arnold, "creaked under the strain. Only a man with the physique of a Greek god and a will of iron could have held on." Mr Potts' toupee slipped forward over his spectacles as he hung grimly on to the liana when it slipped slowly through his muddy fingers and in desperation he clamped his strong Greek god's teeth on it as his expensive boots gave up their struggle and abandoned themselves to their fate. A moment later he arrived at the bank with a sucking, gurgling squelch.

"And so, once again," said the triumphant voice of P. W. Arnold, "Captain Gregory Dangerfield had cheated death and found himself in the arms of a beautiful woman. And as Princess N'Kooma, her magnificent breasts straining like wild Javanese Jakorandi fruits against his taut brown torso, rained hot kisses on his haggardly handsome face the Great Umbala beat his giant fists on his chest and gave a cry of ecstasy that rang through the jungle in a peal of praise for his prowess, with a primitive passion matched only by the pulchritudinous Princess N'Kooma as she entwined herself like a jungle vine in a moment of magic with Greg-ree the white god from the skies."

As Mr Potts received his just reward for services rendered last time, he dropped in on the Frog People, and with the sound of Umbala's fists thudding in time with his overtaxed heart, the scene faded and once again he found himself sitting in front of his washstand at the ancient Imperial typewriter at 69 Ranleigh Road, Streatham.

With a sigh of relief Mr Potts flexed his aching fingers and after bending down to plug in his electric kettle lit a cigarette, sat back and contemplated his reflection. His hair was standing on end, as it always seemed to do after an adventure, and even now it was still hard to believe that the bespectacled face staring back at him belonged not to Henry Potts, writer of cheap detective stories, but to the handsomest man in the world. A fictitious hero, born at the turn of the century on the typewriter of the late P. W. Arnold, whose ancient Imperial now rested in front of Mr Potts. The old typewriter that had become, over the past few months, a magnet, a drug — part of his very existence — for as soon as Mr Potts placed his fingers on the faded keys an unseen force had them tapping away with an unaccustomed expertise, and a Voice, not unlike that of the late George Sanders, a Voice belonging in fact to the late P. W. Arnold, would whisper the beginning of yet another adventure. Then, in a moment Mr Potts would be transported, like Alice through the Looking Glass, from his humdrum existence in Mrs Fiona Harris's boarding house across the barrier of time to the Roaring Twenties to become once again the dare-devil captain. Mr Potts bared his teeth and screwed up his eyes, admiring his reflection in the mirror. Hard to believe that those steely chips of blue ice belonged to mild mannered Henry Potts. In fact, he thought, opening his eyes slightly, hard to see his eyes at all when he screwed them up like that. He tried just raising his bottom lids. No, a bit too Chinese.

The whistle of the kettle interrupted his train of thought and as Mr Potts dropped a Tetleys teabag into his blue mug he wondered what the other occupants of the house would say if they knew of his secret life and that he was really the master of Dangerfield Manor, with a fleet of magnificent motor cars and a faithful manservant called Maltravers, who was in reality the barman at the Rose and Crown. The flamboyant Mr Leopold, in the room below, who had given him his mug for his birthday would probably throw back his golden locks in amazement and recommend psychoanalysis and offer to come with him to hold his hand on the couch! Yes. Little did Mr Leopold realise that, as Vivian of the Merchant Navy, he was Dangerfield's illegitimate son whom he had rescued from the male harem of the White Sultana some months ago. *(See the Further Adventures of Captain Dangerfield)*

Then there was the irascible Mrs Fiona Harris, his Scottish landlady, who had looked after P. W. Arnold in his declining years before he was, to use her own expression, snatched away by the guid Lord, leaving her to recount to the occasionally changing clientele at Ranleigh Road stories of P. W. Arnold's many adventures as a deserter from the Legion, aeronaut, womaniser and general man about the world. In the telling she left little doubt that she had been more than fond of him and that his loss was almost as painful to her as that of her husband, the late Mr Harris, whom she always referred to as "the most famous Baritone". Mr Potts never tired of Mrs Harris' accounts of how, as "the most famous Baritone's" accompanist, she had toured the country bringing the music and gaiety of The Desert Song and Chu Chin Chow, with an occasional excerpt from Cole Porter, to places as far apart as Frinton-on-Sea, Bognor Regis and Ashton-Under-Lyne.

Mr Potts turned and gazed at his pine-framed portrait of "the most famous Baritone", who stared back from the flowered wallpaper, dressed as always in white tie and tails, his small mouth open sustaining some forgotten note under his large moustache. Mr Potts smiled as he remembered meeting Mr Harris only last week, as he had knelt before Dangerfield pleading for his life on the steps of his palace in Peking and how he, Henry Potts, in the role of Dangerfield had pointed a stern finger and sent Mr Harris to work in the rice fields to pay for the indigniaties that Miss B. Catchpole, of the National Westminster Bank, had suffered at his fat Oriental hands. They were hands, that had, before Dangerfield overpowered the four Sumo wrestlers and toppled the giant Jade Buddha that had concealed the door to her dungeon, ripped away Miss Catchpole's coolie shirt causing her magnificent bosom to spring out and wobble tantalisingly in front of Dangerfield before he could politely close his eyes, as he sat bound and gagged at the edge of the snake pit from which he had so miraculously escaped.

And now he was once again back in his room, having a nice cup of tea after being adrift in a balloon and narrowly escaping death in the Javanese jungle. He walked over to his window, opened it, inhaled deeply on his cigarette and looked out at the snow-covered roofs of the neighbouring houses.

Down in the back garden of Ranleigh Road was the snowman with the two pieces of coke placed there for eyes, and the old scarf and hat that Mrs Harris had found in the attic. He'd spotted a pipe up there, but Mrs Harris had informed him that she was sure it had belonged to the late Mr P. W. Arnold and she had indicated in her best Clydeside accent that to use it to decorate a snowman would indicate a lack of proper respect.

The small footprints that criss-crossed the snow covered garden denoted that young Sydney Baldwin, the nine year old son of Mrs Harris's cousin Mrs Beatrice Baldwin, with the bulging hypothyroid eyeballs, who worked as a temporary saleslady in the corsetry department of Pollock Bros. the department store, and who had recently taken over Miss Rumbold's room, had entered the potting shed but had apparently not come out again. That was unless, observed Mr Potts, he had retraced the steps by walking backwards. What was the pale Sydney, who had escaped from the plot of the *Lord of the Flies,* doing, thought Mr Potts. He was not particularly fond of small boys, but Mrs Beatrice Baldwin seemed to pay little attention to him and appeared to spend her time either entering contests in women's magazines, doing the football polls or finding some excuse to knock on his door and enter for a chat about how lonely she was since her husband had left her. Her earnest manner and the way she kept crossing her short fat legs, exposing from time to time black Directoire knickers, left Mr Potts in no doubt that she was desperately in love with him and he prayed she would not appear in one of his adventures and in a moment of madness remove her Directoires and fling her short fat body into his unwilling arms.

If only, thought Mr Potts, she could achieve her ambition and go to Australia to join her sister who, she claimed, ran an English Tea Shoppe in Alice Springs or Wogga Wogga or somewhere in the great outback. Yes, that would be a relief, for Mrs Harris's stern heart had melted when she had heard how the evil Mr Baldwin had run off with the manageress of a launderette in Littlehampton, and how cruelly her sweet cousin, whom she had not heard from for 20 years, had been treated, and who was now divorced and penniless, because of the unfortunate fact that her affair with the milkman (and a part-time window cleaner) had come to light, precluding the chance of alimony. In a fit of generosity Mrs Harris had allowed Mrs Baldwin and the heir to the Baldwin misfortunes to reside rent free at 69 Ranleigh Road until the fare to down under could be raised.

It was a decision which Mrs Harris now regretted as much as Mr Potts, for Mrs Baldwin showed no signs of ever leaving, claiming that her weekly pittance at Pollock Bros. was hardly enough to live on. She looked set to end her days in rent-free comfort unless, thought Mr Potts, she manages to snare some unsuspecting male into matrimony. He shuddered as he thought how dangerous it was for a man to be single and attractive while such woman roamed the earth. Mr Potts already regretted his rash moment yesterday when he had called Sydney to his room and said, "Here's something that might keep you busy, old chap." The pale Sydney had departed with a chemistry set, and a few moments later the Directoire knickers were crossing and uncrossing in front of his eyes as their owner sat on his bed, and he was smiling enigmatically and drinking from the tumbler of warm sherry that Mrs Baldwin had brought with her, as she explained how lucky a man would be to have a ready-made family. When she started to unbutton her cardigan, claiming that central heating was prone to make her dizzy (due to the fact that she had a weak heart), Mr Potts abandoned the enigmatic smile and calling Sydney to his rescue had taken him into the garden to make the snowman.

Now as he gazed at Sydney's one-way tracks he wondered what he was doing down there. Perhaps, thought Mr Potts, he was hiding from his mother. He certainly would have hidden from her had she been *his* mother. In fact, he realised by the way he was creeping about his room that he was hiding from her now, hoping she would think he was out.

He listened, but apart from the occasional creak of expanding woodwork, caused by the central heating, the old Victorian house was as silent as Mr Harris's tomb. He pictured Mrs Harris asleep on her chaise longue, in her private lounge, dreaming of the highlights of her theatrical career, and watching over her prostrate form, from his mahogany frame on the wall, "the most famous Baritone" dressed as the Red Shadow, shading his eyes against the desert sun, ignoring her snores as he peered across the room and out through the front window at the snow-covered hedges of Ranleigh Road.

Mr Potts imagined the anxiety in the eyes of the Red Shadow, for a rival from the past had recently arrived at Ranleigh Road, Signor Alberto Baroli the Basso Profundo and formerly second male lead in the Harris Touring Company. A one-time contender for the slim, exquisite hand of Mrs Harris, and whose name now received first billing on the Bath Rota, indicating that he was a resident at Ranleigh Road and within striking distance of getting his hands on the one thing most dear to his heart. The deeds! The deeds to 69 Ranleigh Road via the now washday red hand of the widow Harris who had to the best of Mr Potts' knowledge so far not succumbed to the Great Basso Profundo's sonorous, crockery-vibrating advances. But, remembering her own words, "It's not easy being a woman alone", Mr Potts had little doubt that the ageing dark, booming-voiced Signor Alberto with his liquid black eyes and splendidly waved, undetachable toupee, would finally pin a flower on the wide lapel of his best pre-war concert suit and march her down the aisle singing, “Thees ees my lucky day”, to the theme music of *Bless the Bride*.

Yes, thought Mr Potts, no wonder the Red Shadow was anxiously shading his eyes, for Signor Alberto would soon return from the dog track, where he liked to spend his Saturday afternoons to continue his assault on the legacy of bricks and mortar for which “the most famous Baritone” had sung himself into an early grave assisted, of course, by the liquid refreshment that his aching tonsils seemed so often to crave.

Mr Potts sighed, yes it was a tricky situation at Ranleigh Road and one that the Late P. W. Arnold, had he been alive, would have rapidly sorted out. For was not the late P. W. the only other man in Mrs Harris's life? Yes, thought Mr Potts, old P. W. would have challenged the saturnine Signor Alberto to a duel at dawn by the potting shed, and disposed of him with a sporting shot through the left kneecap and then by begging or borrowing, or, more than likely, stealing, he would have financed the bloodsucking Mrs Baldwin's trip to Australia or indeed anywhere.

Pity he wasn't in the same mould as that old rogue elephant, thought Mr Potts, with a twinge of regret.

A loud explosion awoke Mr Potts from his reverie and replaced it with the sight of the potting shed minus its windows. As Mr Potts gazed in fascinated horror at this transformation a blackened Sydney appeared minus a lot of hair and holding a hammer. Seeing Mr Potts' white face staring down at him, he shouted triumphantly.

“I've made gunpowder, Mr Potts!” And waving the an' it didn't arf go off wiv a bang.” Mr Potts opened his window.

“Yess, I heard it,” he said, nervously. “Er, you all right, Sydney?”

“Yer” said the small blackened figure in the school blazer.

“What's going on?” said the unmistakeable tones of Mrs Harris, as she appeared in the garden walking on the heels of her carpet slippers. Mrs Harris was followed closely by Elsie, the ex-dresser from the theatre days and now faithful menial and maid of all work. Her curlers bobbed anxiously as she took in the scene.

"Oh my Gawd, 'e's blown 'is 'air 'awf," screeched Elsie, wringing her thin hands in dismay.

"Calm yourself Elsie," said Mrs Harris, and taking Sydney by the shoulders she closely inspected his remains. "You're a very lucky boy," she said sternly. "You could have badly hurt yourself." Then even more sternly, she added, "As it is, you appear to have caused extensive damage to my potting shed, which will have to be paid for."

"I'm sorry, Mrs 'Arris."

"Harris with an aitch," admonished Mrs Harris. "Now, what were you doing to make such a bang?"

"Makin' gunpowder wiv the chemistry set what Mr Potts give me."

"That Mr Potts gave you," corrected Mrs Harris. "I see."

Then, spotting with her eagle eye the transfixed Mr Potts as he peered anxiously from his eyrie, she called, "I shall want a word with you later, Mr Potts."

"Yes, Mrs Harris," said Mr Potts. "I rather thought you would."

Sunday dinner at Ranleigh Road had a strained atmosphere about it. Mrs Harris told Elsie off for not heating the plates properly, and summoned her with the table-bell, half way through the second course, to point out that there was a hair in the steak and kidney pie.

As Elsie wrung her hands in anguish, Mrs Harris picked up the evidence between finger and thumb and swung the piece of meat attached to it hypnotically in front of Elsie's eyes, expressing as she did so the sincere hope that it would not happen again.

The normally gay and flamboyant Mr Leopold appeared to lose all interest in his dinner and visibly slumped in his chair. Signor Baroli cleared his throat and to the accompaniment of vibrating crockery recalled how, during the war when he was touring the Western Desert with ENSA, he had found an ear in some goulash while visiting a Turkish regiment. Only Mrs Harris's commanding hand prevented him from explaining how it had got there; or indeed, how he had even got to the Western Desert. For, if Mr Potts recalled correctly, in a previous story Signor Alberto had never left England. Perhaps a mental aberration had led him to remember a moment from World War I.

At the mention of the severed ear Mr Leopold slumped even further in his chair. The evening had not started well for him; no-one had mentioned the new Fair Isle pullover he was wearing and the limp red and yellow tulips in the glass vase in the centre of the table clashed painfully with its purple and orange pattern. The wretched boy Sydney had placed a small plastic beetle in his soup. Mr Leopold had studiously refrained from noticing it, thereby removing any pleasure his would-be tormentor might have derived, but, unfortunately, while inquiring if that was a new handkerchief that Mr Potts was sporting in his breast pocket (in the hope that Mr Potts would, in turn, notice his new pullover) he had swallowed the plastic beetle. Then, catching Sydney's unblinking eye, he had been forced to continue displaying his lack of emotion which had not been easy as it appeared to have lodged on top of his left lung and, what with the hair in the pie, the awful thing in the goulash was now the final straw.

"I might have an early night," wheezed Mr Leopold, addressing the limp tulips.

"The windows of the potting shed will not be inexpensive to replace," said Mrs Harris to the silver table bell.

"It was very hot in the desert," boomed Signor Alberto to the mustard pot.

"I find the heating very hot in my room," complained Mrs Baldwin to the tomato sauce bottle. Then she switched her protruding eyes on to Mr Potts and gave him a meaningful stare.

I expect she's trying to tell me she lies in her hot room, attired only in her discount knickers, hoping the picture will excite me, thought Mr Potts with a shiver. Then aloud he said "The potting shed was my fault, Mrs Harris. I shouldn't have given Sydney the chemistry set."

"'e's eaten my beetle," muttered Sydney, glaring accusingly at Mr Leopold. "What beetle?", wheezed Mr

Leopold bravely.

"I'm sure you meant well, Mr Potts," said Mrs Harris. "It's just that I've had a lot of bills lately. It's not easy being a woman alone," she said, using her favourite phrase. "Nor a man," breathed Signor Alberto.

"It was different when 'the most famous Baritone' was alive," continued Mrs Harris. She turned and looked at the late Mr Harris who gazed back from his small silver framed picture on the sideboard and apologised, with a cheery wave from the stage door of the Brighton Pavilion, for not being there to suffer with her.

"A wonderful man," boomed Signor Alberto, placing his large hairy-backed hand on Mrs Harris's arm and gazing at her with his liquid eyes. "Aye," said Mrs Harris, "he was that."

There was what seemed to Mr Potts an awkward pause, but apparently Signor Alberto was unaware of it. Taking a deep breath and raising his napkin in a dramatic gesture he sang, "You'll never walk alone". The captive audience hardly had time to applaud before he launched into "Eef I ruled the world, every day would be the first day of sprreeng, every heart would have a new song to seeng . . . " while staring into Mrs Harris's eyes.

Mr Potts mentally changed the lyrics to "Eef I get the house, everyone will be out in the street . . . " and as the great Basso Profundo continued, Mr Potts gazed interestedly at his quivering jugular vein and red face. He wondered if the heat of his self-induced blood pressure would melt the glue securing what must be the most magnificently coiffured toupee with its subtle touch of grey at the temples. Mr Potts had, on a number of occasions, tried to detect the join but he had to admit that without the aid of a magnifying glass it was impossible to see. Nevertheless no-one, Mr Potts told himself, had that much magnificent black wavy hair at Signor Baroli's age.

As the plates and cups clattered and bounced, Mr Potts fixed an appreciative smile on his face to match that of Mrs Harris and after trying unsuccessfully to avoid Mr Leopold's eyes, which rolled up in exaggerated dismay indicating his anguish, he joined in the applause. "Magnificent," said Mrs Harris. "Absolutely magnificent, Signor Alberto, You have lost none of your range."

"Thank you Fiona," gasped Signor Alberto, clutching his heart and breathing heavily. "But when one is inspired . . . " he waved his napkin about in her direction before carefully applying it to the beads of perspiration below his hairline.

"I am definitely going to turn in early," said Mr Leopold, striking his chest with a sharp blow with his fist. "We've had a terribly busy week at the Salon, I hardly had time to go out to buy this new Fair Isle sweater."

"The beetle in your soup . . . deadly poisonous," hissed Sydney.

"Time you were in bed, Sydney," said Mrs Baldwin.

"Agreed," said Mr Leopold.

"Say goodnight to everyone," said Mrs Baldwin, as she rose.

"G'night," said Sydney.

"*Go*odnig*ht*," enunciated Mrs Harris clearly.

"Goodnight," said Mrs Potts as the Baldwins headed for the doorway.

"Farewell sweet prince," boomed Signor Alberto.

"Good riddance," gasped Mr Leopold.

"Now then," admonished Mrs Harris, "boys will be boys." Then she sighed. "We were all young once," she informed the cheeseboard.

Mr Potts felt a twinge of sympathy for the vast lady in black bombazine, whose ornamental comb, a relic of her role in *Chu Chin Chow,* had failed to secure all her swept up dyed black hair, several strands of which hung lifelessly down as she gazed morosely at a small piece of Stilton and some crumbly Camembert. "What you need, Mrs Harris," he said, "is a holiday."

"Do you know," said Mrs Harris, stabbing the Stilton, "that I have not had a holiday for these past 25 years."

"Almost before I was born," said Mr Leopold.

"I don't mind not having a holiday," said Mrs Harris, "but I've had quite a drain on my financial resources recently . . . "

Mrs Baldwin, thought Mr Potts.

". . . and," continued Mrs Harris, plucking at a stray strand of hair, "what with repairs to the house and the increase in prices, due I suppose to us joining in with the Frogs as the late Mr Harris used to call our French cousins, I'm just a wee bit down. In fact," she added, in a low voice, "I've even thought of selling Ranleigh Road."

"No," said Mr Leopold, his lips twitching with horror. "Not 69 Ranleigh Road." "That is our address, I believe," said Mrs Harris.

"You could do worse," said Signor Alberto, with what Mr Potts recognised as a persuasive smile. "It would fetch a good price. Then you could live by the sea, a small bungalow, perhaps with a close friend or companion and then, with the money, you could travel."

As Signor Alberto continued, and suggested that travelling alone was unwise, Mr Potts interrupted: "Surely not. This house means so much to you, Mrs Harris. I'm sure things will get better."

"Yes," said Mrs Harris recovering her composure. "Yes I'm sure they will. Now, who'd like some sherry?"

"Me," said Signor Alberto holding out his glass. "When I get all the money my agent, whose whereabouts are unknown, owes me, I will take you on holiday," he lied.

And Mr Potts knew at that moment that if old P. W. Arnold had been alive he would have begged, borrowed or stolen to see that his beloved Mrs Harris was relieved of her financial worries and that Mrs Baldwin would be despatched without delay. And if there was any way he could arrange it himself, he would. But how? Little did he know that P. W. Arnold was thinking along the same lines as he hovered over the mantlepiece on the other side of the Veil.

Mr Potts had just wrapped his pyjamas round his hot water bottle and popped the striped bundle into his bed, before making his cocoa. when he heard a tap at his door. His heart sank.

"Yes," he said, adopting the quavering voice of someone already half asleep. The door opened and Mrs Baldwin's protruding eyes expressed delight at catching him in time.

"I'm glad I caught you in time," she said. "I wanted to give you this." She held up a brown envelope and waving it like a pass, she entered his room and closed the door behind her.

"What is it?" said Mr Potts, unscrewing the lid of the cocoa tin and resigning himself to his fate.

"Well," said Mrs Baldwin, as she sat on the edge of his bed, "I'm not having any success with my draws lately and wondered if you would like to have a go?" Mr Potts gave a start of alarm and remembering the fate of the milkman and part-time window cleaner put an extra large spoonful of cocoa in his cup.

"I'm always so unlucky," said Mrs Baldwin, crossing her Directoires with a provocative swish, as Mr Potts stirred his cocoa vigorously, "And suddenly thought," continued Mrs Baldwin, "Why not let Mr Potts have a go . . ."

No wonder Mr Baldwin left, thought Mr Potts and measured the distance to the door, as Mrs Baldwin rose.

"And so . . . " said Mrs Baldwin. ". . . I'll leave this pools coupon with you and wish you luck." And placing the brown envelope on Mr Potts' bed and giving him a final hypnotic stare with her protruding eyes, she left as swiftly as she had arrived.

Pools coupon! Mr Potts breathed a sigh of relief and took a large sip of cocoa, pulled a face and added the spoonful of sugar that the unnerving conversation had caused him to forget.

Opening the envelope he carefully studied its contents. Mr Henry Wordsworth Potts had never considered that he possessed enough luck to enter a competition, but the happy faces of previous winners that stared up at him from the back of the Vernons coupon headed "For a Friend" reminded him that nothing was impossible. Just unlikely!

He read the instructions carefully: he had to pick out eight drawn games. Perhaps if he imprinted the names of all the teams firmly in his mind he would dream of the results as he slept; yes, that sort of thing did happen occasionally. Then he remembered that he had a bad memory. Well, why not try, perhaps if he typed them out they would stay firmly imprinted in his mind. Yes, that's what he'd do, and sitting down in front of the old Imperial typewriter he reached for the white sheet of foolscap the top of which already contained the final details of his adventure in the Javanese jungle. But before he could touch it an unseen force caused his fingers to fly like homing starlings to the faded keys, and after a moment of intense activity he read the words they had typed.

"The awful Mrs Baldwin is going to Australia — and the sooner the better."

"I agree," said Mr Potts. "But when? And How?"

"It's quite simple," typed his fingers. "You are going to send her there."

"Me!" said Mr Potts. "How on earth . . . ?" But before he could continue, his busy fingers rattled out the answer like a machine gun.

Arsenal
Chelsea
Crystal Palace
Aston Villa
Blackpool
Bolton
Port Vale
Aberdeen

Mr Potts stared at the names for a moment, then as their significance sank in, he looked up and said "It's the pools. I'm going to win the pools."

The names seemed to glitter in gold as he gazed at them. He, Henry Wordsworth Potts, was about to be rich and his happy face, with an ear-to-ear grin, would soon be staring at new friends from the back of a pools coupon, and out of the winnings he was going to get a second class ticket to deport the Baldwins. He would ignore the begging letters and with the rest of the £100,000 . . .

"Not that rich," typed his fingers with a staccato burst. "As a matter of fact," continued the keys, "you are going to win £642.10. "It's a bad week," they added, "lots of winners".

"Couldn't we wait for a good week?" said Mr Potts hopefully. "Look here," snapped P. W. Arnold's voice in his ear, and his busy fingers confirmed the news, "I had great difficulty in finding out this information. Winning the pools is not exactly considered as a matter of pressing importance on the Other Side, you know."

"No, I imagine not," said Mr. Potts hurriedly, "and I'm extremely grateful to you for helping me."

"I am," typed the keys, "more concerned with helping my dear friend Mrs Harris, who has been under some strain of late. Not only from the attentions of that bounder Baroli, but she has been giving money to her cousin, whose tale of hard luck seems to be unending and indeed I fear it is."

"I understand, leave it to me," said Mr Potts. "Oh and by the way, P. W., I enjoyed my last adventure very much indeed. Really thought I'd had it when I fell in the swamp."

"So did I," typed his fingers. 'Damned careless of you. Still, I must admit you are getting better at being Dangerfield. In fact, I've had a most intriguing idea for your further adventures. But more of that later. Suffice it to say that I have enough confidence in you to pit you as Dangerfield against the greatest villains the world has known."

Mr Potts felt a feeling of great pride swell in the area of his breast-pocket handkerchief, followed by a twinge of anxiety. "Er, thanks, P. W." he said cautiously, and waited for a reply. None came, so taking a sip of his tepid cocoa and producing his best biro pen, he carefully marked eight crosses on the coupon "For a Friend" against the teams picked out, with the ethereal assistance of the Late P. W. Arnold.

The following week seemed to last a month and Mr Potts had great difficulty in refraining from telling Mrs Harris that some of her major problems were about to be solved and that he was about to win on the pools. He had also considered putting crosses against the same teams on Littlewoods, Zetters, Copes and a couple of the other pools firms' coupons, but at the back of his mind was the thought that perhaps P. W. Arnold didn't want him to win too much, and might somehow insert a phantom feather up a goalkeeper's shorts at a critical moment if he got too greedy. After all, £642.10 when he had an overdraft at the National Westminster of £11 was not to be sneezed at.

During the week he'd made a number of attempts to contact P. W. again to have another adventure as Dangerfield and so pass the time quickly. But, meeting without success, he had decided to finish his latest detective story about an undercover agent whose true identity, hidden under the guise of Betty, a blonde chorus girl, was not to be revealed until the last page. Putting aside the worrying thought that the title, "It's a Fair Cop," might give too much away to the reader, he finished it the following Thursday morning and after a splendid kipper and tomato lunch in the kitchen, during which he caught up with William Hickey's social scene in Mrs Harris' *Daily Express,* he took a bus to the High Street and mailed his manuscript at the Post Office to his publisher's P.O. box number and buying a postal order, from a dark gentleman with frizzy hair (who could easily have been a member of the Frog People), he carefully filled it in and put it in the brown envelope with his winning coupon to Vernons. As an afterthought, he approached the section of the counter marked "Registered letters and parcels" and tapped a coin on it to indicate he was there.

This time a very attractive brunette girl appeared and, giving him a flashing smile, took his letter and registered it under his watchful eye. As she bent over and drew crosses with her blue pencil, he was able to admire the way her short brown hair was attractively tinted blonde at the ends and by bending his knees slightly he could cast a surreptitious glance down the front of her open-necked blouse. The sight of the edge of her black bra and a half hidden safety pin made his whole afternoon worthwhile and put him in such high spirits that he decided to vist the bank and demand to see the manager. Of course, he wouldn't tell him he was going to win the pools. He'd just say that he, Henry Wordsworth Potts, would like to extend his credit facilities, just up to say £20 or indeed fifty. He would point out, just in case it had slipped the manager's attention, that money must be kept circulating to keep the economy going and if the manager refused to help the economy . . . ?

Mr Potts narrowly avoided being run down by an irate taxi driver as he wandered across the road practising the enigmatic smile he would allow to play across his mouth should the manager be so shortsighted. Then next week he'd pay in his winnings and just as the manager had fallen to his knees thanking him profusely, he'd close the account and take everything out again, and let it be known that he was on his way to Barclays and exit with a Dangerfield gay laugh, leaving behind a wailing and gnashing of teeth, particularly from the red headed Miss B. Catchpole of the tellers' counter. He suspected she was secretly in love with him, not just because he had rescued her from Mr Harris in Peking, but the flashing smile she gave him when he made his last withdrawal had, he felt sure, been full of hidden meaning. Perhaps he should ask her out. But perhaps not until he'd paid in his winnings, then the word would spread around the bank and she'd realise he was a good catch.

As Mr Potts strode through the portals of the National Westminster he reminded himself that to think Dangerfield was to be Dangerfield and with a smile of contempt on his lips he marched up to the enquiries counter, rang the bell twice and banged sharply on the counter with the flat of his hand. Then, quickly feeling with his finger, he made sure his top lip was curling sardonically up at the corner.

Miss Catchpole who had observed his entrance from behind her teller's window nearby, stood on tiptoe to get a better view of Mr Potts.

"Blimey," she murmured to herself, "old 009221 'as 'ad a stroke. 'is top lip's gone all funny."

Then, in her best banking voice she called out, "The Inquiries is still at lunch, sir. Can I help?"

For one moment Mr Potts was thrown off his guard and his stern lip relaxed into a warm smile. "Oh, hello, Miss B. Catchpole," he said. "Didn't see you there."

As he spoke Miss Catchpole disappeared from view behind a partition then reappeared in front of him. Standing face to face with Miss B. Catchpole always made Mr. Potts' heart thump so loud he was sure she could hear it and raising his voice to hide the sound he answered in a stentorian bellow that he would like to see the manager. Then, remembering the role he had to play, he raised his top lip back into its sardonic snarl.

Mr Potts' sudden changes of expression reminded Miss Catchpole of the spine-chilling Dr Jekyll and Mr Hyde movie. With a nervous smile and using a soothing tone, she murmured, "Just wait there sir, I'll get him right away."

Mr Potts recognised the shy smile she gave him before she backed away and leapt so quickly out of sight as one belonging to a girl who is strangely attracted to a member of the opposite sex. He must try being forceful more often. Mr Potts was in the middle of practising a strong forceful look that combined an attractive smile when Miss Catchpole returned closely followed by the grey haired manager. Mr Potts curled his top lip back hurriedly and stuck out his jaw. Miss Catchpole gave a gasp that Mr Potts recognised as admiration, then she shyly leapt out of sight again behind the manager's broad back.

"Yes, Mr Potts," said the manager.

"I'd like," said Mr Potts, finding speaking with a jutting jaw and curling lip less easy than he'd imagined. He continued with a gruff lisp, "I'd like to discuss credit facilities."

The manager stared at him keenly for a moment and Mr Potts was aware that Miss Catchpole was peering over the manager's shoulder. He relaxed his face for a moment, gave her a smile, then resumed his stern expression, obviously most effectively as the manager was slowly backing away with an anxious look on his face.

"Of course, Mr Potts," he said in a low, calm voice.

"Up to £20," lisped Mr Potts gruffly.

"No trouble," said the manager as he and Miss Catchpole backed out of sight. "No trouble at all."

Suddenly the Inquiries area was deserted and Mr Potts decided that the manager must have had to return to a meeting. "Thanks," he called. He looked round for Miss Catchpole, but she was just erecting a "Closed" sign at her window. Mr Potts wondered whether to ask her for lunch, but decided to wait until he'd paid his winnings in, then they could go to the private bar at the Red Lion.

As Mr Potts walked down the High Street he decided that the National Westminster wasn't such a bad bank after all and buying Sydney a copy of *Beano,* which was the only comic he could remember, and regretting that Wilson the

Wonder Athlete had disappeared from its pages, he returned to Ranleigh Road in high spirits.

Saturday afternoon found him buying a bottle of Italian champagne at the wine shop to celebrate his win and keeping up his strength with a bar of Cadbury's fruit and nut, he stood by the newsstand outside the tube station, as he waited for the arrival of the sporting edition of the *Evening Standard*, which would confirm his and Mrs Harris's good fortune.

Despite his woollen scarf, wrapped twice around his neck, and two pairs of socks, he soon found he was shivering with cold. Pulling down his scarf and pushing the last of the chocolate in his mouth he clapped his hands and stamped his feet to keep his circulation going, thinking how nice and warm the Javanese swamp had been and how pleased he would be if Dangerfield's next adventure took place in a ladies' Turkish bath. At that moment two things happened. An elderly lady, leaning heavily on a walking stick, mistaking him for the newsvendor asked him in a tremulous voice for a *Knitting Weekly*. At the same time a piece of silver chocolate paper lodged in one of Mr Potts' back fillings causing his nerves to inform him that he was in mortal agony. He thrust his gloved finger into his mouth and gave a low animal cry as he prodded about with great urgency. The elderly lady indicated that the *Knitting Weekly* was of little importance and striking at those in her path hobbled off at great speed into the gathering gloom.

"If I haven't won," muttered Mr Potts through his chattering teeth as he opened the paper at the bus stop, "I'll have a few words to say to . . . " He tailed off as his eyes caught sight of the results on the back page. He was still staring at them as the human tide carried him on to the bus.

Mr Potts entered into the familiar aroma of floor polish and potted plants and closing the front door of Ranleigh Road quietly behind him (Mrs Harris could not bear the sound of a banging door) and filling his lungs, he announced, with a force that made the aspidistra plant tremble, "I've won! I've won the pools!"

"I've won the pools," echoed his voice around the hall. "The most famous Baritone" stared at him with open-mouthed surprise from his place next to the barometer.

The voice of Mrs Harris came faintly from her private lounge. "What's all that shouting?" she said.

Mr Potts picked up the dinner gong from its stand, and ignoring the fact that it was sacrosanct, having been used by the late Mr Harris in the touring version of 'The Desert Song', he beat it with great abandon and shouted, "Whoopee."

"Mr Potts," said Mrs Harris sternly, as she entered the hallway, "Have you taken leave of your senses? Only I am allowed to sound that gong."

"Don't tell me the house is on fire," shrieked Mr Leopold, as he ran down the stairs two at a time in his best pink terry-towelling bathrobe. "I've won the football pools," said Mr Potts, pointing to the paper. Mr Leopold stopped in mid flight, jaw open. "No," he said.

Taking the gong and giving it a quick polish on her ample posterior, Mrs Harris carefully replaced it on its stand together with the stick and held out her hand. "Let me see," she said, putting on her reading glasses that hung from the black ribbon round her neck.

"Here," said Mr Potts, handing her the paper and producing his copy coupon from his inside pocket. He waited tensely as she checked the results.

Mr Leopold crept down the hall, bringing to Mr Potts' nostrils the strong aroma of *Brute pour les Hommes*. Mrs Harris clicked her tongue as she mouthed the names of the teams. Then she nodded and smiled, then she did something she had never done before, except in a Dangerfield adventure; she put her vast arms around Mr Potts and kissed him warmly on the cheek.

"Congratulations. I'm so happy for you," she said clapping her hands together in delight. "Oh well done," said Mr Leopold, giving Mr Potts a hug with his pink towelled arm. "How much?"

"Probably not a fortune," said Mr Potts guardedly. "It varies you know." And once again Mrs Harris's vast arms drew him to her bosom, and as Mr Potts received his second congratulatory kiss on the other cheek amidst the aroma of mothballs and eau de cologne that fought for supremacy with *Brute,* the front door opened and a familiar voice boomed across the hallway.

"What ees thees I see?" "You'll never guess what, Signor Baroli," shrieked Mr Leopold, "my friend Mr Potts has won the pools."

"No," cried Signor Baroli, closing the door behind him and removing his vast black ankle-length overcoat. "No," he repeated, throwing his hands up in a theatrical gesture to indicate disbelief, surprise, and pleasure. Then he clenched them to add a hint of sadness that he had not won the pools himself.

With the same difficulty, Mr Potts refrained from applauding this display and nodded. "Yes," he said casually, "got eight draws up. We're just going to celebrate."

"Magnifico," said Signor Baroli, carefully removing his hat. Taking Mr Potts' hand, he pumped it vigorously up and down. "Magnifico," he repeated. Then, pausing, he inquired in a sepulchral whisper, "How much?"

"Probably not a fortune," said Mr Leopold. "It varies you know."

"This calls for a wee drink," announced Mrs Harris. "Come into my private lounge and I'll open by best Port which I was saving for Christmas."

"A splendid idea," boomed Signor Baroli.

"I bought this when I found out," said Mr Potts, not untruthfully producing the bottle from his pocket. "Champagne," he added.

"Oh, an Italian one too," said Mr Leopold.

"The best," said Signor Baroli.

"I'll get the glasses," said Mrs Harris. "Unfortunately Mrs Baldwin is still at the store, but we'll save some for her." And like some vast ship under full sail, she turned on her heel and headed for the Port in her private lounge.

Some time later, when an exhausted Mrs Baldwin had returned from her labours at Pollock Bros, and young Sydney had been sent to bed after returning from a Scout meeting (where, apparently he had passed his fire lighting test so successfully that Streatham Fire Brigade were still fighting to save Scout headquarters), the tenants of 69 Ranleigh Road, after consuming the Port, champagne, an ancient bottle of Advocat and a large bottle of cooking sherry (of which Mr Potts had had a not inconsiderable amount to fortify himself against Signor Baroli's varied selection from *Faust, Carmen* and finally "Ol' Man River" that had reduced Elsie to uncontrollable sobbing', were called to order by a flushed Mrs Harris.

As she rose from the piano, which vibrated from the pounding of her still nimble fingers, she held up her hands in a commanding gesture that had never failed to stop the chatter under a sea of raffia hats before the curtain up at the Concert Hall.

"Friends," she said, "this is indeed a splendid day, and I only wish my late husband, 'the most famous Baritone', was with us to share it. And if everyone is agreeable I would like to propose a toast to him." She raised her glass. "To the most famous Baritone," she said. "Most famous Baritone," chorused Mr Potts and the others, solemnly raising their glasses.

"And to his beautiful widow," added Signor Baroli raising his glass. And with appropriate murmurs the others followed suit, though they hurriedly lowered them as Elsie fell from the chaise longue alternatively crying and laughing hysterically.

When order had been restored Mr Potts cleared his throat and clutched the piano for support. The cooking sherry and Italian champagne seemed to have made him light headed and he had slight difficulty in focussing his eyes. "And now," said Mr Potts, "I would mike to lake an announcement. Er, . . . like to make, I mean."

"Quiet for Mr Potts," boomed Mrs Harris theatrically as she held up her hands.

"Quiet in the hall," boomed Signor Baroli.

"You're making all the noise," said Mr Leopold, swaying slightly, apparently unaware that his pink dressing gown had fallen open to reveal his purple "Y" fronts. Elsie, from her sitting position on the chaise longue, had noticed, and hurriedly stuffing her hanky in her mouth struck her knee several times with her head.

Mrs Baldwin put her arm round Mr Potts and appeared, to his discomfort, to be gazing admiringly directly up his nostrils with her protruding eyes, which seemed to swim in front of his like two blue jellyfish. Trying to ignore her, and clearing his throat again, Mr Potts continued.

"I have," he said, choosing his words very carefully, "been very fortunate in winning the pools." "Hear, hear," agreed Signor Baroli.

"Lucky," said Mr Leopold. "Very lucky. But you deserve it." "You're a wonderful person," breathed Mrs Baldwin up his nose and her arm gave him an extra squeeze.

" . . . And," continued Mr Potts, after taking a deep breath, "I've always wondered what I did if I do . . . er, . . . what I'd do if I did . . . " He noticed that his voice seemed to be coming from a long way away. "You're not leaving, are you?" inquired, Mr Leopold anxiously.

"No," said Mr Potts.

"Good," breathed Mrs Baldwin.

" . . . And I think," said Mr Potts, "that there is someone here, a lady, who has not been fortunate lately . . . "

"There is," whispered Mrs Baldwin.

". . . That lady," continued Mr Potts, "is the unfortunate Mrs Baldwin . . ."

"She has indeed been unfortunate," said Mrs Harris. "Left alone with a wee bairn to raise and no-one to turn to . . . "

" . . . And with a weak heart," said Mr Leopold sadly.

There was a pause following this brief resume of the Baldwin misfortune.

"Er, yes," said Mr Potts, losing his thread slightly. Then juggling mentally with what he had to say, he heard his voice continue. "And I, as you know, have no dependants. I am alone . . . " "You've got friends," hiccupped Mr Leopold, absentmindedly pulling aside his dressing gown and scratching his bottom. "Friends you can trust."

Elsie bowed her head and buried it in a cushion and hammered the back of the chaise longue with a clenched fist.

"What I'm trying to say," said Mr Potts, through the foggy haze that was closing in on him.

"I think I know," breathed Mrs Baldwin excitedly.

" . . . is," continued Mr Potts, "that, I propose . . . "

But Mrs Baldwin's sudden fierce grip round his middle prevented him from continuing his intended words "to pay Mrs Baldwin's passage to Australia, because it's better to help those less fortunate, etc.", and to his ears came the most frightening words he'd ever heard, even as Dangerfield. For, like the knell of doom, Mrs Baldwin's voice rang in his ears.

"I accept," she said. And before Mr Potts could think how to phrase his denial, she continued with breathless excitement, "Oh, I knew you wanted me. I knew, I could tell, Oh, Mr Potts you've just made me the happiest woman in the world." And with that Mrs Baldwin threw her arms round his neck and as his mouth fell open in horror and surprise, she pursed her lips and kissed him passionately on his front teeth.

His legs suddenly assumed the consistency of rubber bands, and as though in the grip of some inescapable nightmare he felt Signor Baroli pumping his limp hand up and down and felt Mr Leopold slap him on his back. Then, as though in a trance, he heard Mrs Harris say how lucky Mrs Baldwin was to get such a good man. His last recollection, as he started to fall, was the picture of Mrs Baldwin's hypothyroid eyes gazing at him adoringly, and as Elsie started to sing "Walter, Walter, lead me to the altar", merciful oblivion overtook him and with a jangle of assorted notes he bounced off the keyboard of the baby grand and into the alcoholic arms of Morpheus.

When Mr Potts came to he was in bed, he had a pounding headache and wondered why he couldn't remember getting there. He sat up and placed a hand on top of his head to prevent if taking off. Then he remembered. The pools win. The drinks. The speech. The misunderstanding. Mrs Baldwin hadn't taken him seriously. Mrs Baldwin *had* taken him seriously! He must leave the country immediately. No, just a moment. What would Dangerfield do? Dangerfield would do the gentlemanly thing. He wouldn't leave the country, he'd just shoot himself or perhaps something more dramatic liking driving himself, at the wheel of his Bugatti Royale, over Beachy Head saluting at the wheel. Dangerfield, of course. This was all P. W. Arnold's fault making him win the pools, and now, instead of getting rid of Mrs Baldwin he was engaged to her. Married to Mrs Baldwin. Mr Potts shuddered at the thought.

Mr Potts switched on his bedside light and with a shaky hand lit a cigarette, then looked at his watch. Twelve-thirty, and good heavens, he was in his pyjamas. Surely Mrs Baldwin hadn't been allowed to put her bridegroom-to-be to bed. What a liberty! But perhaps he had got into his pyjamas himself and just couldn't remember. Yes, that was more like it.

Then, to his horror, Mr Potts noticed that his pyjama cord was tied in a reef knot. He always used a bow. So whose hand was that? The answer came in a flash — hadn't Mr Leopold been a sea cadet? Yes. It was Mr Leopold's hand. He mustn't drink again, ever. He dragged heavily on his cigarette. Or maybe he should drink and Mrs Baldwin would realise that she had made a grave mistake. Mistake — that's it. Perhaps he could tell her it was a mistake. He imagined the confrontation.

"Er, Mrs Baldwin. Excuse me. I made a mistake. I just wanted to give you enough money to leave." Mrs Baldwin clutches heart and dies. No, not the best way to put it. Damn old P. W., he'd got him into this so he could jolly well get him out of it.

Mr Potts threw back the covers, put on his dressing gown and, placing his spectacles on his nose, sat gingerly down in front of the ancient Imperial typewriter and contemplated his pale face, distraught hair and red rimmed eyes that stared worriedly back at him.

"P. W.," he said sharply. "Where are you?". And like homing starlings his fingers leapt to the keys. "Your a fool Henry," they typed. The Late Author's Voice confirmed his lowly opinion of Mr Potts. "A damn fool."

"Your fault," said the aggrieved Mr Potts.

"A couple of drinks" rapped the keys, "and you're up to your neck in trouble. Still there's many a slip twixt cup and lip, or I'd have been married a dozen times."

"It's all right for you," said Mr Potts. "You're dead. And if I don't get out of it, I'll be joining you."

"Heaven forbid, well, for the time being," tapped the keys, "You see, Henry, you can't be Dangerfield up here so you've got to stay there."

"I don't," exclaimed Mr Potts, "think that I am too concerned about being Dangerfield at the moment . . . "

But the keys cut him short. "Don't worry," they typed, "I'll think of something." "Promise," said Mr Potts hopefully. "You have my word" said the voice of the late P. W. Arnold and the keys confirmed the promise in heavy type. "I'm relying on you," said Mr Potts sternly.

"And now," continued the Voice in time with the printed word, "I have interesting news. I am at this very moment with none other than the late Sir Arthur Conan Doyle.' Mr Potts felt a surge of excitement flow through his body and for a moment his troubles fled. This was a dramatic turn of events for an avid reader of the *Occult News.* "No," he breathed. "Yes," rattled the reply. "And," continued the Voice proudly, "he has consented to allow me to pit Dangerfield's remarkable prowess against Sherlock Holmes' arch enemy, the Napoleon of crime, Professor James Moriarty."

Mr Potts gave a gasp of apprehension. How would Dangerfield fare against such an evil villain? Even old Holmes with his massive intellect had had to spent a lot of time scraping away at his violin while he mapped out his next move against the master criminal.

"Are you sure I'm quite up to it?" inquired Mr Potts anxiously, lighting another cigarette from the stub of the previous one.

"We'll see," rattled the keys, "Sir Arthur has specially written the plot, which I will dictate to you."

"What, now!?" queried Mr Potts. "But I have an awful hangover. I'm not sure I'm up to it."

"Dangerfield," typed his fingers, "does not have a hangover and is at the peak of physical fitness. Escape into his world, Henry Potts, and become once again a man of action. As you walk along the fog-shrouded pavement of Baker Street, on your way to number 221B to meet the most famous detective of them all . . . "

A thought struck Mr Potts. "Hang on P. W.," he said,

"what date, year, does this story take place?" "Eighteen ninety nine," clacked the keys. "But," said Mr Potts, "my other adventures took place in the nineteen twenties. How old am I supposed to be? I mean," he added, "I must have been a boy at the turn of the century."

There was a pause, then his fingers rattled off an astounding piece of news. "The time has come," he typed, "to let you into a secret, hitherto known only to me." Mr Potts stared expectantly at his poised fingers. "Gregory Dangerfield," they typed, "was born over two centuries ago." "Good Lord!" whispered Mr Potts. "But how does he manage to stay so young and handsome?" Mr Potts' mind flashed back to a previous adventure when he had disposed of evil Dr Carl Frank, the longevity expert. Had Dangerfield known all along about the glandular secretion of the Bora Bora Turtle that was supposed to prolong life?

"Because," said the voice of the late author, "as a young man he made an expedition to a hitherto hidden valley, known only to the late Rider Haggard, and there fell in love with the Goddess Ayesha, known locally as 'She', who took him unflinching into the eternal flame of youth." And then in capital letters he typed. "CAPTAIN DANGERFIELD CAN NEVER GROW OLD."

"No, really," said Mr Potts, and sitting back he breathed a sigh of relief. At the same time he felt a tinge of regret that he couldn't remember that heated moment long ago with Ursula Andress's predecessor, but what good news, and of course that explained why Dangerfield's favourite weapon was a silver duelling pistol, by William Binns & Son of Noneaton; he'd probably used it in the days of the late Jeffrey Farnol, author of *The Amateur Gentleman,* in the days when charm wasn't at a premium and chivalry was taken for granted.

Now, by means of the old Imperial, he could still be youthful, handsome Dangerfield, until he, gnarled old Potts, could no longer type.

"That secret is safe with me, P. W." he murmured.

"I know," he typed. "And naturally," added the keys, "it allows us to have adventures ranging from staring into a basket in the French Revolution to saluting the Red Baron as you plunge out of control in World War I."

"Absolutely," agreed Mr Potts enthusiastically. Then as an afterthought he added, "and landing safely on friendly soil despite the bullet holes in my tail."

"Something like that," murmured the Voice vaguely. "But let's hurry or you'll be late for your appointment with Sherlock Holmes!"

"Right, P. W." said Mr Potts. "I'm ready."

And as his fingers typed him into the past the sound of the ancient keys died away to be replaced by his own echoing footsteps and Mr Henry Potts found himself without a hangover walking purposefully along the famous street in Victorian London.

Two

"Piper, paiper — read all abhart it," screeched a reedy, cockney voice in the gloom ahead.

Mr Potts jumped with surprise, then steeled his Dangerfield nerves. He always took a moment to get into an adventure and suddenly finding himself in cold, foggy London after his warm room at Ranleigh Road took a moment to get used to. He suddenly saw ahead of him a small urchin, wearing an overlarge cap at a jaunty angle. The pale, underfed face told him that young Sydney had not had to change his grammar or appearance to play the part of a seedy newspaper vending youth.

"Jack the Ripper slashed anuvver young girl to deaf," screeched Sydney. " 'Orrible murder."

The small figure clutched his sleeve with a grimy hand and thrust a paper at him. Cuffing his stepson-to-be over the ear and ignoring the stream of abuse, Mr Potts hurried on with a shiver. He must be mad walking through London on a foggy night with chaps like the Prince of Wales, or whoever the Ripper really was, leaping about killing everyone. Then he remembered with a sigh of relief that it was only young women that the Ripper did to death.

"Spotting 221," said the welcome voice of P. W. Arnold, "Dangerfield entered and, handing his hat to Mrs Hudson, told her he must see Holmes immediately." Handing his smart, curly brimmed bowler to Elsie, whom he was not surprised to meet in the menial role of Mrs Hudson, he announced that he wished to see Mr Sherlock Holmes. "Yes, sir," said Mrs Hudson. "This way sir. Mind the stairs sir." And knocking at the sturdy door and popping her head round, she announced as she had done in so many stories before. "There's a gennleman to see you, Mr 'Olmes."

"Enter," said a compelling voice.

"In here, sir," she said.

"Thank you, Mrs Hudson," said Mr Potts as he stepped through the doorway into the famous study. His eyes took in the acid-stained deal-topped table, the row of formidable scrapbooks, the pipe racks. Yes, and there was the violin case and even the Persian slipper in which old Holmes kept his tobacco, and behind a cloud of blue smoke was the great man himself. Mr Potts gave a gasp of surprise as the smoke dispersed. He had not expected to meet Mr Leopold so soon or playing such a leading role in the plot. For, although the hair was now dark and swept back and he seemed even thinner and his nose protruded like a hawk's beak, it was undoubtedly the occupant of the room below his at 69 Ranleigh Road who wore the long red dressing gown with black lapels and who spoke in a deep, cultured voice.

"We have a visitor, Watson," it said. Definitely on the ball thought Mr Potts as he stood in the doorway. A grunt near the fireplace, in which a small fire burned brightly, drew Mr Potts' attention to the other occupant of the room. Slumped in a comfortable chair was the late Mr Harris, wearing a bushy white moustache and a Norfolk suit. Mr Harris blinked his eyes in surprise at the sight of their visitor.

"What the devil, Holmes," he spluttered, "who is the feller?" Mr Potts mentally noted that he had preferred Nigel Bruce in the part.

"Unless I'm mistaken," said Mr Leopold puffing nonchalently at his meerschaum pipe, "he is an ex-army man and has spent a great deal of time abroad. He is an exponent of the deadly Kemelman Nerve Hold and the art of Thai foot fighting and possessor of perhaps the fastest reflexes in the world. He is adored by women and is a deadly shot. He has in the left inside pocket of his jacket a letter that was delivered by hand this very evening. Apart from that I know nothing about him."

Mr Potts was deeply impressed, there was no doubt that Mr Leopold would have given Basil Rathbone a run for his money. He felt in his jacket pocket and, yes, there was a letter.

He pulled it out and glanced at it.

"But how the devil," said Mr Harris in his bumbling Watsonian voice and waving his arms about. "How the devil could you tell?" "Elementary my dear Watson," replied the great detective. "Good evening Captain Dangerfield."

"Dangerfield, the adventure feller?" waffled the figure by the fireplace. "Well I'm damned, how did you know?"

"Yes, how?" said Mr Potts as he sat down in the vacant wing-backed chair that the tall figure indicated with a wave of his pipe. "Easy," confessed the pale, hawk-nosed Leopold. "I read an account of your exploits in this week's *Strand Magazine,* which also carried your picture, sir, and as far as the letter is concerned, for a man of your considerable abilities to visit my chambers at this time of night can only mean a matter of the utmost importance and that some-one's life is at stake. If it were your own, you would deal with the matter yourself. Therefore, someone has communicated with you by hand, otherwise had a missive been delivered in the post you would have visited my chambers much earlier in the day and as I perceive, by the nicotine on your index finger, that you are right handed the letter would logically be in your left inside pocket to be least vulnerable to a passing pick-pocket. May I ask the lady's name?"

"Even Dangerfield," said the admiring voice of the late P. W. Arnold, "was impressed by Holmes' perspicacity and handed over the missive." Mr Potts handed Mr Leopold the envelope he found in his pocket, noticing as he did so that he was wearing a smart checked suit, "specially tailored," murmured the voice of his creator, "by Reginald Jinks and Son of Ludgate Hill. The buffalo hide boots are by the Hudson Bay Trading Company, and the shot silk shirt by Sheiki's of Singapore." Immaculate as ever, thought Mr Potts.

"What's it say, Holmes?" inquired the figure by the fire. "Dearest Gregory," read the vibrant and clear voice of the master detective, "unless you come to Rake Manor, Wimbledon, before midnight, alone — I am to die. Signed, Lady Lavinia Browning."

Typical Dangerfield situation, thought Mr Potts. Beautiful women in trouble, writing to the man they loved. But why had he come to see Holmes, why hadn't he just jumped into a horse-drawn bus and galloped over to Wimbledon?

"Now why," said Mr Leopold, tapping the letter thoughtfully with the stem, of his meerschaum pipe, "why would Lady Lavinia Browning, the rich recluse, need your help?"

"Dangerfield," said the voice of the late P. W. Arnold, "was puzzled, for he'd never met the lady."

"I've never met the lady," said Mr Potts, "which is why I came to your chambers."

"There can only be one answer," said the astute Leopold, running his fingers lovingly over his violin case. "Indeed Holmes, and pray what is that?" inquired Mr Potts drumming Dangerfield's slim, brown fingers on the arm of the chair to remind those present that he was a man of action.

"That she is to be killed," said the detective, rolling up his left sleeve and revealing a thin, pale, undernourished arm.

"Good God Holmes," said the late Mr Harris, "how do you know?" Mr Potts realised that if Conan Doyle hadn't invented Watson a lot of questions would have gone unanswered. "Simple," said Mr Leopold dabbing his thin arm with a piece of cotton wool, on which he had poured something from a small bottle. Probably got a boil on the way, thought Mr Potts. Probably a bit run down after *The Speckled Band* and, of course, *The Hounds of the Baskervilles* must have taken a lot out of him.

"A rich woman who is a recluse," said Mr Leopold obviously relishing his role as a mastermind, "is unlikely to commit suicide. Therefore, if she is to be killed, so that some person or persons unknown to us at present . . ." he paused significantly and picked up, to Mr Potts' horror, a hypodermic from the desk, " . . . can," he continued, "come into her vast fortune, then it must be made to look like suicide. An accident would be suspected immediately." "Of course," snorted Watson. "Damned clever."

"The greatest proportion of suicides are women," said the great detective, plunging the needle into his arm, causing Mr Potts to wince anxiously. "And," he continued, pressing the plunger, "women in love."

A smile of relief crossed Mr Leopold's pale face as he withdrew the needle. Junkie, thought Mr Potts. Of course, he remembered now, old Holmes was always having a quick shot in the arm or a sniff up the aquiline nostrils to keep him going.

"But if I've never met her?" said Mr Potts. But as he spoke the thin figure suddenly collapsed into a chair, eyes closed and chin resting on his chest. Given himself an overdose and gone, thought Mr Potts. But as he half rose from his chair the voice continued. "Why?" it said, speaking into its dressing gown, "because they fall in love with you and there you have the key." The eyes opened and stared brightly at Mr Potts. "Yes, it's all quite clear," said Mr Leopold leaping up and pacing excitedly up and down the worn Indian carpet. "Yes, yes of course! But how?" And opening the violin case he took out his beloved instrument and tucking it under his pale chin, he drew the bow across the protesting strings.

Mr Potts winced and prayed that inspiration would come quickly. "Ah, got it!" shrieked Mr Leopold, leaping in the air with excitement. Placing the violin on the table he paced up and down in an agitated manner, which Mr Potts recognised as typical of Holmes in the grip of a brainwave.

"It all fits," he exclaimed, "she is to commit suicide with her secret lover."

"And who, my dear Holmes," said Mr Potts patiently, "is her secret lover?"

"None other than the one man who would be sure to drive her into a frenzy of despair, the handsomest man in the world. None other than, sir, you sir. Captain Gregory Dangerfield."

"Me?" said Mr Potts. "But I've never even met the lady."

"Exactly," came the exasperated reply. "That's why I say secret. No doubt a note in her own handwriting will confirm the affair and your bodies will be proof of it."

"Our bodies?" said Mr Potts uneasily.

"What a devilish plot, surprised I couldn't see it myself," breathed Mr Harris, through Watson's bushy moustache.

"Fascinating," said Mr Leopold. "Come on Watson, we have work to do."

"What's that, Holmes?" said Mr Harris. "But dammit, Dangerfield's safe here. Without him she can't be killed."

"But," said Mr Leopold, taking a revolver from a drawer in his desk and peering down the barrel, "to arrest the miscreants we must have a crime, or an attempt, and for that purpose Dangerfield must go to Rake Manor ahead of us and at the *moment critique* we will strike."

Mr Potts decided that whatever was in the hypodermic it wasn't doing the great detective a lot of good. But before he could protest, the voice of his creator, the late P. W. Arnold, spoke for his ears alone. "And so," intoned the Voice, "the gallant Captain Dangerfield found himself in a hansom cab, as it approached the forbidding manor house on the edge of the common, standing like a sentinel under the dark scudding winter clouds, through which the raging moon peeped palely.

"I'll bet Conan Doyle didn't write that last paragraph," thought Mr Potts as he found himself jogging uncomfortably in a small horse-drawn cab through the swirling evening mist. This was quite a different sort of adventure. Perhaps not so fantastic as his previous ones but, by its seeming reality, more frightening. Overcome by his enthusiasm to become Dangerfield again and escape from the dull surroundings of Ranleigh Road and the thought of his impending nuptials, he had rashly entered into mortal combat with the deadly Moriarty. Damn! He should have told Holmes that his arch enemy, the Professor, was behind the plot, but perhaps the hawk-nosed Holmes already suspected it. He turned and peered through the small back window of the cab, but to his dismay saw no sign of another containing the indomitable Duo. The next moment he heard the sound of gravel under the trotting hooves and on looking out saw they had arrived outside an imposing front door.

"'ere we are sir," said the becapped, mufflered driver, and the red nose glowed familiarly in the oil lamp sidelights, it was Bill the barman from the Rose and Crown.

"That'll be sixpence sir," said Bill touching the peak of his cap, and holding out a blue hand. Mr Potts felt in Dangerfield's trousers and pulled out a handful of loose change and in the lamplight he saw the shine of real silver shillings and even a five shilling piece from which Queen Victoria's profile stared sternly. "Here you are, fellow," he said in a commanding voice and tossing the coin into the grateful, servile hand, he leapt out of the open door, a move which turned out to be a grave error of judgement, as he had not realised how high off the ground hansom cabs were.

Striking the heel of his buffalo hide boot on the protruding footstep, he fell head first at the feet of the surprised lackey, whose outstretched helping arm he had so coolly ignored.

"What the devil's your man doing?" A surprised ethereal Voice that was unfamiliar to Mr Potts.

"Please don't interrupt, Doyle, replied P.W. Arnold, then continued. "With great presence of mind," he murmured admiringly, "Dangerfield threw himself on the ground to avoid the possibility of an assassin's bullet catching him unawares."

Assassin's bullet? Mr Potts rose cautiously, he must be very careful. But the house seemed empty. Was he at the right address? Well, there was only one way to find out, and crunching his way up to the front door, he searched for the bell.

The warning voice of the late P. W. Arnold stopped him. "Sensing a trap," said the Voice, "Dangerfield, moving with the speed of a Venezuelan viper's tongue, darted round the corner of the house to seek a side entrance."

Good old P. W., thought Mr Potts, as he leapt for the flower beds and flattened himself against the ivy-covered wall. Of course, he was right. Moriarty was a tricky customer. If he was going to rescue Lady Lavinia he mustn't take chances. I wonder who she is, thought Mr Potts, with luck she might be the blondish brunette, with the black bra, at the Post Office, living as a recluse and waiting to unleash her pent-up passions in the arms of the handsomest man in the world. After risking a foggy foray in the wilds of Wimbledon.

"Suddenly," said the familiar Voice in the darkness, "Dangerfield's eyes, keener than those of the Guatamalan goggle-eyed gull, spotted an open scullery window."

Mr Potts, who had backed round the side of the house as the author spoke, banged his head painfully on the open window that his goggle gull eyes had failed to notice and, losing his balance, sat down with a bump as the window slammed shut.

"Has your man been drinking?" inquired the Voice of the late Conan Doyle.

"Clumsy," hissed P. W. Arnold accusingly.

"Sorry," said Mr Potts and then, to his horror, he saw a light go on behind the window and leaping hurriedly to his feet he ran back through the mist the way he had come.

Suddenly, without warning, he was face to face with a dark figure that stood with a heavy looking cane raised about his head. "Good evening," said a deep resonant voice that had so recently sung 'You'll a-never walk alone.'

"It was," said the worried voice of Dangerfield's creator, "the face of the master criminal himself, Professor James Moriarty, the most ruthless criminal in the world." And as though to confirm this Signor Baroli struck Mr Henry Potts forcefully on the head causing him much pain and the last thing he remembered was digging Dangerfield's strong, handsome nose with great force into the damp flowerbeds.

Mr Potts came to with a headache, far exceeding in magnitude the hangover he had escaped by entering the story of Dangerfield's latest escapade. His hands were tied behind his back and secured to a metal ring on the cold stone floor on which he was sitting. Also, his keen Dangerfield nostrils detected the unmistakeable smell of burning. He was to be burnt alive! What horror! And without even meeting the heroine and sharing a last moment with her. His eyes peered through the darkness, but even with Dangerfield's keen vision he could discern nothing.

He mustn't panic. After all it was only a story and he, or more correctly Dangerfield, had got out of tighter spots. But where was Moriarty, alias Signor Baroli? And more important, where was Holmes? Mr Potts started to cough. The smoke was getting thicker. How much longer could Dangerfield's magnificent lungs hold out? He coughed again. It was getting lighter and suddenly, as though waking from a dream, he was back at Ranleigh Road, sitting at the typewriter in the old washstand. And there was smoke everywhere.

Mr Potts came out of his momentary trance and saw the

cardboard box that served as his wastepaper basket was smouldering busily by his feet. Of course. The cigarette he'd lit when he'd started the story. It must have dropped in there and now he had a fire on his hands. Leaping up, he poured the remains of the water in the kettle on to it and stamped frantically with his foot at the smoking remains, realising too late that he was not wearing his carpet slippers. With great alacrity and clutching an injured toe, Mr Potts hopped round his bedroom giving vent to a howl of agony before finally collapsing on his back on the bed. Pulling his foot as near to his mouth as he could, he blew on it with great vigour.

A knock on the door, followed by the door opening before he could reply, followed by Sherlock Holmes, the worse for drink and wearing flowered pyjamas, momentarily took his mind off his misfortune. Then realising that it was, of course, Mr Leopold as himself, he waved towards the washstand and gasped, "Sorry to wake you, had a fire, burnt my foot." "Oh, my word," said Mr Leopold, clapping a hand to his cheek in horror. "You might have been killed. I'll open the window."

Mr Potts resumed blowing as Mr Leopold steered an unsteady course for the window and threw the offending remains of the wastepaper box into the garden. "There," he said triumphantly. "It's all safe now." Then turning he said, "I hope you didn't mind me bursting in like that. "Of course, at first, when I heard the commotion, I thought I'll bet Mr Potts is entertaining Mrs Baldwin. But when I heard her snoring across the passage, I thought I'll bet all's not well up there with Mr Potts. So I came to see."

"Thank you," said Mr Potts.

"Not at all," said Mr Leopold, his lips twitching sympathetically. "Here, let me see." And before Mr Potts could protest Mr Leopold took hold of his foot in his well-manicured hands and examined it like a botanist examining a rare plant.

"Only a little one," he pronounced. "Nice feet too," he added admiringly. Mr Potts hurriedly retracted his foot.

"I'm fine now," he said. "It was just a shock."

"Let the air get to it," advised Mr Leopold.

"I will," said Mr Potts. "Goodnight."

"Sleep tight," said Mr Leopold. "I know I will." And with

that he staggered out of sight noisily, slamming the door behind him, causing Mr Potts to place his hand on top of his head to prevent it leaving again. Which reminded him of his hangover and his betrothed, who for the moment, was snoring alone. But unless he could think of a way out, apart from plastic surgery to disguise himself and join Martin Bormann in Brazil, she would soon be snoring much nearer to him.

He shuddered at the thought, then consoled himself that the old campaigner, P. W., had promised to think of a way out. And thinking about ways out, what had that evil Moriarty got in store for the brave Captain Dangerfield? What a fool he'd been to get caught so easily. Fancy letting P. W. down like that. Maybe he was losing his grip. He certainly hoped not. Well, there was only one way to find out, and at the same time forget the pain in his toe and the banging in his head, and that was to return to the scene of the crime and trust to his instinct for survival, escape and claim his grateful prize.

As Mr Potts tied his best hanky round his toe he sighed. Pity he hadn't got a regular girl himself, then he wouldn't have to keep careering round the world to get his hands on the lovely heroines who always attended Dangerfield's adventures. Still as Dangerfield he had met a great variety of ladies and for a bachelor in a bedsitter, in Streatham, he wasn't doing too badly. And Princess N'Kooma of the Frog People had been most grateful, although more primitive than he would have preferred.

After tidying the pages that he had typed in his somnambulistic state he inserted a fresh sheet of foolscap into the ancient Imperial and resisting the temptation to light another cigarette, consigned himself to his fate. A moment later, like the twitching of a hazel twig in the hands of a diviner, his fingers leapt to the keys and as they tapped away the hammers in his head disappeared to be replaced by giant mallets crashing away inside his skull, as he found himself once more sitting on the same floor of his prison.

"But even though," said the admiring voice of the late P. W. Arnold, "Captain Gregory Dangerfield had been bound while unconscious his phenomenal reflexes had automatically caused him to expand the muscles of the wrists in the manner taught to him by the Giant Achmed Ackbar (known as the Titanic Turk), whose boast 'No prison bars shall hold me, nor will I die in chains' was indeed prophetic and his sudden death choking on a boiled sweet, which he had taken from a young boy, was a sad blow to the underworld of Istanbul."

Mr Potts tugged hopefully at his bonds but they seemed very secure. Perhaps his wrist muscles hadn't gone down yet. Then, out from the darkness, he heard a voice that caused him to breathe a deep sigh of relief. "There is little doubt," said the crisp, decisive voice of Sherlock Holmes, "that Dangerfield is a prisoner."

"Maybe the feller escaped," mumbled the welcome voice of Watson, "and has gone for help."

"I'm here," called Mr Potts. "Tied up. Quick before old Moriarty gets back!" Good old eagle-beaked Holmes, he thought. Found me first go.

"Hurry up," he added anxiously, as he waited for a reply.

"Hold on," said the Voice. "I'm just trying to strike a match with my feet and it's not easy."

Had Holmes gone bonkers? thought Mr Potts. Perhaps that shot in the arm had made him a bit light headed. And then after a gasp of effort in the darkness a match suddenly flared, revealing to Mr Potts a disturbing scene. Both Mr Leopold and his inseparable companion were also prisoners and each was tied with hands behind back and the two ropes that ran round their waists disappeared into the darkness above.

It was immediately clear to Mr Potts, by the light of the match that Mr Harris held grimly between his teeth and the matchbox held between Mr Leopold's feet, that they were lucky to have any light at all and only by Conan Doyle's hero, athletically swinging on his rope like a gymnast, had this momentary glimpse of their predicament been possible.

By the flickering light Mr Potts noticed a number of large wine barrels nearby, indicating the possibility that they were in a cellar of some sort situated in the bowels of the house.

"I fear Captain, we are all in the same boat," said the pale Mr Leopold in an even voice that displayed not a tremor of fear. "An apt phrase, as it happens," he continued, "as I observe the arrival of water from an inlet behind the gallant Captain's head." Water? Yes. Mr Potts could hear it gurgling behind him. Good heavens, they were going to drown. He looked anxiously at the Great Detective who then turned to his faithful companion, who still held the lighted match grimly between his teeth.

"I suggest," he said, "that a quick blow, Watson, may save you having to diagnose the degree of incineration your proboscis is about to suffer, and will almost certainly save you from having to grow another moustache."

"What? Oh yes," mumbled the medical millstone and with a lot of puffing and snorting managed to extinguish the match.

Mr Potts' mind was racing overtime and the answer it came up with was rather comforting, if Sherlock Holmes was also a prisoner his creator Sir Arthur Conan Doyle was hardly likely to allow him to die at the hands of Moriarty or how would Holmes be able to dispose of his arch enemy in a later adventure? It was only Dangerfield that this villain was pitted against, so as long as they stuck together all was well.

"What the devil!" exclaimed Watson's voice. And to Mr Potts' surprise the voice seemed to float down from him in the darkness. Then, also from above, a light appeared revealing to Mr Potts' astonished eyes that both Watson and Holmes had vanished into thin air and he was alone in the walled room. The floor was already submerged beneath the cold water, that was, even now, soaking his superbly cut trousers. Then, silhouetted against the light, he became aware of the tall sinister figure of Professor James Moriarty who was, conceded Mr Potts, at this moment in the story, considerably ahead on points.

"Goodbye Dangerfield," he said, his deep voice reverberating round the walls of Mr Potts' prison. As this was not the first time a villain had uttered a hopeful farewell to Captain Gregory Dangerfield, Mr Potts gave his usual teeth-bared, light bantering smile of derision in reply.

"Dangerfield," said the voice of the late P. W. Arnold, "gazed up with his steely blue eyes, the quality of crystal quartz, eyes that had outstared the effeminate Ling Po, as he had worked with fiendish cruelty on Dangerfield's left ear. Now these eyes held a glint of derision as they gazed up at the evil Moriarty." Mr Potts blinked Dangerfield's unusual eyes and tried to get them used to the darkness.

"You are probably wondering why you are to die," said his adversary, indicating to Mr Potts that his deductive powers were on an equal footing with those of Holmes.

"It did cross my mind," said Mr Potts, trying to make his voice sound nonchalent with even a hint of flamboyance, which he knew would please P. W. on the spiritual sideline.

"It is because," came the answer, "you are considered by women to be the handsomest man in the world." Ah, thought Mr Potts, of course, he's jealous. It's the big forehead that puts them off. Then aloud he said, "So?"

"So," replied the sombre voice of the silhouette, "it will come as no surprise that Lady Lavinia threw herself into the Thames in the arms of her lover, and her note, written in an undetectable facsimile of her writing, will confirm that you, Captain Dangerfield, were indeed her secret admirer and that jealousy prompted her to pull you from a punt to your double doom at Thames Ditton. Her vast fortune will then go to those who are in my control. Do I make myself clear?"

Crikey, thought Mr Potts. The cunning swine. Old Holmes had been right. But where was Lady Lavinia? Poor girl, probably drowned already before they had a chance to meet and console each other in their final moments. Pity, he'd like to have had a quick go at her before he went. But, of course, he wasn't going. He would escape, but how?

The figure disappeared and suddenly the squeaking of ancient machinery above his head came to his ears. Looking up he saw the bound, struggling figure of a woman being lowered directly over his head. Mr Potts breathed a sigh of relief. Lady Lavina was still alive and by the reflection of the light in the water he was able to see up her long skirt, but apart from the fact she was wearing long expensive-looking knickers, in keeping with her reputation as a rich recluse, he could see nothing of her face because of the angle of descent.

But he did see something above the bound figure that made him gasp with surprise. It was the feet of Holmes and Watson as they hung suspended over his prison, soon to be grave.

"I'm afraid," echoed the voice of Mr Leopold from his eyrie, "that for once I have underestimated our adversary."

Just my luck, thought Mr Potts. Then with Dangerfield's traditional bravado he called out, "Don't worry, Holmes. We'll get out of this somehow."

"How dammit?" called the inquisitive chronicler of Holmes adventures. Pity, thought Mr Potts, that old Holmes hadn't made friends with a brain surgeon instead of a local G.P.

His thoughts were interrupted by a splash, as the bound figure of Lady Lavinia arrived at its destination. Held by the rope, she hung in a sitting position swaying in front of Mr Potts' sympathetic gaze. Her head was slumped on her bosom and her long tresses hid her face, but the moan that escaped from her invisible lips informed him that the cold water was reviving her from the faint that Victorian ladies were prone to in times of stress.

"Be brave, Lady Lavinia," exclaimed Mr Potts in a strong gritty hero's voice. The head slowly raised and the tresses fell back and the enormous blue, protruding eyes opened and stared hypnotically at him. Now it was Mr Potts' turn to be brave, for the woman he was to die for was none other than his bride-to-be at Ranleigh Road, Mrs Baldwin!

"Who are you?" she gasped. "Captain Dangerfield at your service," replied Mr Potts morosely, adding with sadistic pleasure, "and we are about to die." "Dangerfield," breathed Mrs Baldwin clutching his arm, "Oh thank heavens." To his relief the protruding eyes instantly closed and the head fell forward again.

What a swizz, thought Mr Potts. All very well being pitted against an arch villain, but only worth it if the heroine was young and grateful. They normally had bulging bosoms, not bulging eyes! He must have a severe word with P. W. about that when he got back. But how was he going to get back? For, as the late P. W. Arnold had pointed out once before, if he failed to survive the adventure by losing his nerve or making a fatal mistake that the late author couldn't rectify, he, Mr Henry Wordsworth Potts, would be found dead with his nose buried in the keys of the ancient Imperial typewriter and a verdict of strain and overwork would be recorded at the Streatham registrar's office.

By now the water was rising quite rapidly and was approaching his armpits. "Has it occurred to you, Moriarty," called the calm voice of the suspended Mr Leopold, "that my good friend Inspector Lestrade will have an autopsy conducted on the bodies of your victims and that when the water in their lungs . . . "

Mr Potts felt faint at the picture.

". . . is analysed," continued the calm voice, "it will be found in content to be different to that of the river at Thames Ditton?" "Dammit, why didn't I think of that?" grumbled the late Mr Harris.

Yippee, thought Mr Potts, thanks to Holmes' busy brain old Moriarty had been thwarted. Well, at least for the moment. But it might take him days to think of another plot and by then P. W. Arnold would have thought of a way out.

"An excellent observation, my dear Holmes," boomed the silhouette above the rising waters. "But naturally the thought had occurred to me and a Bellinghurst fire-fighting machine that was advertised for recently in the 'Wanted Column' of *The Times* — an unusual request that apparently escaped your eye — was purchased by myself for the very purpose of conveying the Thames Ditton water to Wimbledon. I think that answers your question."

It certainly does, thought Mr Potts gloomily. Fancy Holmes missing that advert and not putting two and two together.

"If only Dangerfield could get at the knife strapped to his left forearm," said the urgent voice of P. W. Arnold. Mr Potts gave a start of surprise. Knife? Fancy him not noticing it. He tugged again at his bonds. Good, good old P. W., he thought, so Dangerfield had something up his sleeve after all. To his delight he felt his wrists turning and with a final effort he managed to slip them free. Keeping his arms behind his back he pushed his right hand up his left sleeve and felt something hard. Yes, it was there. As he worked to free it from its fastenings, the voice of Dangerfield's creator came through again.

"Freeing," said the Voice, 'the trusty knife, given to him by the cripped Red Indian chief One Toe, in return for saving the life of his daughter, Little Rain, whom he had found dying of thirst in the Navajo Desert, surrounded by a score of prickly green poisonous prairie spiders, whose ability to leap on each others back and pose as a cactus plant has fooled many an unwary traveller, Dangerfield,' concluded the author, 'waited his chance.'

Perhaps thought Mr Potts, Chief One Toe had also taught him to throw it with unerring accuracy and he was about to do Moriarty a great mischief. But as no such information was forthcoming from beyond the veil, he decided not to try in case he missed, thus incurring the arch criminal's displeasure and possibly painful retaliation.

"I am," announced the evil silhouette above Mr Potts, "saving Mr Holmes and the good Dr Watson for a fate that will preclude their interference into my affairs forever. But that is to take place later. Now, before I say farewell, have you anything to say to the gallant Captain Dangerfield, Holmes? Before I close the trapdoors to spare you the sight of his struggles?"

"Only this," shouted the still confident voice of Mr Leopold above the sound of running water.

Mr Potts strained his ears attentively for the words of hope.

"Goodbye sir," shouted Mr Leopold. "I pray your death will be swift and remember in the final count the miscreant will be caught. Of that I assure you." "Yes, goodbye sir," echoed Mr Harris. "Damn proud to have met you." Very comforting thought Mr Potts.

"I have," continued the voice of the great detective, "examined every conceivable way in which you could escape from your predicament, even if you were to free yourself from your bonds . . . "

"Yes?" said Mr Potts alertly. " . . . it would still," concluded the Voice sadly, "be impossible to escape."

And as Mr Potts rose slightly with the tide, endeavouring at the same time to give the impression that he was still bound to the floor, the evil Professor James Moriarty began to close the vast wooden shutters that would seal his doom.

A square of light remained over Mr Potts' head, through which the rope supporting the inert body of Mrs Baldwin (Mr Potts found it hard to think of her as Lady Lavinia) hung suspended. As Mr Potts gazed helplessly up into the last ray of light he would see, he heard footsteps on the wooden roof of his prison and the head of the silhouette appeared.

"It was nice to have met you, sir," boomed the voice of his last and unfortunately successful enemy. Then producing a knife, he cut the rope causing Mrs Baldwin to flop on her back in the water, and the trapdoor closed with a dull thud shutting out the light.

Victorian manners, thought Mr Potts, in a detached way, could be most aggravating. He stood and placing an arm under the thrashing figure, spoke in a low calm voice. "Lady Lavinia," he said, "I'm afraid I have bad news."

"Help," screamed Mrs Baldwin, uncalmed by his tone, and Mr Potts could imagine her protruding eyes almost popping out on stalks as she peered panic-stricken into the gloom. Then, standing, she escaped from his grasp and stumbled off, calling, "Police! Help!"

"Dangerfield," said the urgent voice of the late P. W. Arnold, whom Mr Potts was mentally preparing to meet face to face, "had to work quickly. He must find a wine barrel and remove the bung."

Good idea, thought Mr Potts, as he waded about. Get drunk and ease the awful fate that the stupid old fool P. W. Arnold had got him into. Finding one, he pulled at the protruding bung. It came out quite easily and the smell of wine as it flowed out to join the rising tide reached his nostrils. Not just your usual vin ordinaire, thought Mr Potts, as he licked his fingers appreciatively. Dangerfield was obviously to depart in style.

"Draining the contents into the water," urged P. W. Arnold excitedly, "Dangerfield replaced the bung and prepared his escape." Escape! Mr Potts' blood raced round his veins cancelling out the cold. P. W. had thought of a way, but how?

"And taking," continued his saviour and friend, "the rope that had bound Lady Lavinia . . . " The author paused as Mr Potts' hands scrabbled in the water to find the rope. Finally he found it and pulled. A scream came from some distance away and his catch pulled against him. Mr Potts struggled in the dark to wind in the bulging-eyed, floundering Mrs Baldwin who, despite his soothing words, fought like a fresh water salmon in the peak of condition, until finally tiring, his catch gave up and floated in front of him moaning and thrashing feebly in the rising water.

"Be calm," he said in a stern voice. "We have little time." To his relief at the sound of his voice the lady appeared to have taken refuge in a faint and her inert body floated by his side as he undid the rope around her waist and waited for his instructions.

"Taking the rope," commanded the Voice, "Dangerfield dived under the water and slipped it through the iron ring in the floor."

Mr Potts ignored the diving bit and cautiously felt first with his foot. Finding it, he took a deep breath and slipped the rope through.

"Tying it to the barrel," said the inventive P. W. Arnold, "Dangerfield secured it and waited for his moment."

By now Potts was swimming on his back supporting Mrs Baldwin's head above the Thames Ditton water and then with a stroke of the pen, or more accurately a new paragraph in the story, P. W. Arnold used poetic licence to take the tale on in time.

"And so," said the Voice, "with the rough wooden roof of his tomb only inches above his handsome head, as he supported the barely conscious Lady Lavinia with his strong right arm . . . "

Mr Potts bumped his handsome head painfully as he glanced up to check that time and tide had not waited and had complied with the plot. It had and his strong right arm was locked round the bulging eyed Mrs Baldwin, whose plight was causing him so much discomfort, and at that moment he disliked her more than ever.

The Voice continued, "... Dangerfield murmured an encouraging word to Lady Lavinia and, saturating his magnificent lungs with oxygen, gripped Chief One Toe's knife between his strong white teeth, teeth that had smiled at death before, and dived to the floor of the cellar and cut the rope that held the barrel.'

"Hang on, Popeye," shouted Mr Potts. "How dare you!" gasped Lady Lavinia. But before she could protest further Mr Potts took a deep breath and dived. It seemed an age before he found the barrel and as he severed the rope he wished he'd stayed in bed at Ranleigh Road and started the story when he was feeling better.

Suddenly the rope parted and the barrel disappeared upwards like a bullet, dragging him up in its wake. His head broke the surface just in time to see the barrel had left the water with great force and had burst through the trap door, allowing the light to flood in on his upturned face. A deep cry of dismay reached his ears and as he gripped the edge of the wooden platform and pulled his head clear he saw that on its descent the barrel had struck the evil Moriarty as he stood busily taunting the helpless Holmes and Watson.

"It's a miracle," spluttered Holmes' companion, "but how the devil . . .?" "It's logical," replied the great detective, "and the use of Archimedes' principle as a *modus operandi* for escape is something I had overlooked and I must for once concede to an intellect comparable to my own."

"And," said the pleased voice of P. W. Arnold, "as the triumphant Captain Dangerfield helped the grateful Lady Lavinia from the sinister cellar Sherlock Holmes, the master detective, realised that here was a worthy ally of law and order and that at last the evil Professor James Moriarty had met his match."

As the scene faded, Mr Potts realised that the late P. W. must have read his thoughts regarding Mrs Baldwin and had spared him her amorous gratitude, for in a trice he was back in his room at Ranleigh Road, lighting a much needed cigarette and breathing a sigh of relief at his narrowest escape of all. He wondered, as he clutched his hot water bottle, how Holmes and Watson would escape and after deciding that that was Sir Arthur Conan Doyle's problem, not his, he fell into an exhausted sleep.

The next morning dawned crisp and bright and even reminded Mr Potts that it was nearly Christmas. As he lay on his neat white pillow he allowed his mind to wander back to the time when he was small and had lived with his grandmother, Mrs Potts having passed on after giving birth, while Mr Potts senior had apparently been too busy working to look after his son. Mr Potts remembered hearing that Mr Potts senior was a business man who had to travel to work every day from London to Manchester. He had been most impressed until he discovered that his uncommunicative parent was a restaurant car attendant on the London Express. In fact, Mr Potts had never met him until grandmother's funeral, where his father arrived the worse for drink, smoking a cigar and driving a mobile canteen.

But it was the pillow that triggered off his reminiscent frame of mind, for years ago on cold crisp Christmas mornings he would awake and find a big double pillow case full of toys and games that would arrive mysteriously in the night and cause his heart to beat with great excitement. And now, he sighed, it would be a toilet requisite from Mr Leopold, and the usual diary from Mrs Harris, and new socks and underpants from himself. No, Christmas was not worth looking forward to after you were nine.

Then he remembered Mrs Baldwin and wished he were nine again. Fancy old P. W. casting her as the heroine of his triumphant battle of wits with Sherlock Holmes' arch enemy. And as he had done before, he wondered if his adventures were all just in his own mind and if P. W. Arnold really existed as an entity, but rescuing Mrs Baldwin could hardly come under the heading of wish fulfilment. Then an interesting thought struck Mr Potts. There was a way to find out if P. W. Arnold really was communicating with him, for had he not claimed he was in contact with the late Sir Arthur Conan Doyle? Yes. And Mr Potts recalled as an interested reader of the *Occult News* how Sir Arthur, who himself was in his latter years a devout believer in life after death, had left a sealed envelope behind, the contents of which he had promised to reveal should he ever be able to communicate from beyond.

Mr Potts threw back the clothes and got out of bed. Here was a chance to find out once and for all if he was just imagining that an unseen hand was writing his adventures, or was it really him subconsciously seeking escape from his humdrum world? He would ask P. W. to ask Sir Arthur what was in the envelope and if he couldn't tell him . . .

Mr Potts put on his slippers and sat excitedly in front of the ancient Imperial.

"P. W." he murmured, "calling P. W. Arnold. Are you there? Come in."

The suddeness with which his fingers leapt to the keys almost took him by surprise, and they leapt up and down with great force.

"I am not," said the familiar irate Voice, in time with the keys, "too pleased about being called up in the manner of a ham radio operator. Of course I am here."

"Sorry," said Mr Potts humbly, "but I have a question to ask and I was rather anxious to get a reply."

"What is it?" clattered the keys.

"Er, is . . . said Mr Potts after noisily clearing his throat, " . . . is Sir Arthur still about by any chance?"

"Of course he's still about," snapped the voice.

"I wanted to ask a question," retorted Mr Potts.

"Shoot," he typed. Mr Potts took a deep breath, this was it.

"What," he said, "is in the letter he left that was not to be opened until he came back and said what was in it?"

"I'll ask him," said the voice in time with the keys, "then we can start another adventure."

There was a pause, during which Mr Potts decided he'd made a grave error in probing too deeply into the occult, for if Sir Arthur couldn't tell him then this whole thing was just a figment of his imagination and knowing this might well break the spell and be the end of his adventures. Not only that, but if P. W. Arnold was just a figment of his imagination, his promise to find a way of getting Mr Potts out of his forthcoming marriage to Mrs Baldwin was hardly likely to be fulfilled.

He was about to say never mind, I don't want to know, when his fingers leapt to the keys, but this time he found he was using only the forefinger of each hand and was typing very slowly.

"Good day, Mr Potts," he typed, and with his heart beating excitedly, he realised in a flash that he was actually in direct contact and he half rose from his chair and bowing his head politely replied, "Good morning, Sir Arthur."

As the message was slowly tapped out, Mr Potts read the words with growing interest. "You may remember," he read, "that the late Charles Dickens passed on at the age of 58, having completed Chapter 23 of *The Mystery of Edwin Drood.* Since then many eminent writers of detective stories have tried to solve the seemingly insolvable mystery. Before I died I wrote Sherlock Holmes's deduction of the case of how, in his view, the story was intended to be resolved. Upon my arrival here, I naturally enough, being not an entirely unknown writer, met Mr Charles Dickens and was pleased to hear that my man Holmes had once again unravelled a mystery that has and is still puzzling some of the best brains in the world of crime and detection. I was, however, made to give my solemn promise that I would not reveal the contents of the letter until such time as the best living writer detectives had given up and then, and only then, can I come back and allow my version to be read. I trust this secret is safe with you and I remain, Yours faithfully, Sir Arthur Conan Doyle."

"You can rely on me, Sir Arthur," said Mr Potts earnestly. He sat back and let out a long low whistle of excitement. Of course Sir Arthur's secret would be safe with him, in fact he was surprised, as a detective story writer himself, that he hadn't guessed. Still G. K. Chesterton and others had failed, so he mustn't be too hard on himself.

Mr Potts was just about to rise when his fingers leapt back to the keys and drummed out the words, accompanied by the business-like tones of the hovering P. W. Arnold.

"What about the next adventure?"

"Apart from the fact," said Mr Potts testily, "that I have not had my breakfast yet and did not enjoy the last one at all . . . "

"Mrs Baldwin was ideal for the recluse," rapped the keys.

"No doubt," replied Mr Potts, "but you promised to get me out of the mess I'm in and I don't think I can concentrate on our adventures until you do."

"Oh really?" rattled the reply, and the Voice adopted a steely quality.

"Well, may I inform you, Mr Potts, that I have contacted five great authors over here, all of whom condescended to allow me to use their villains, and there are four left who have been working on plots to tax Dangerfield's remarkable powers and I do not intend telling them that my man does not feel up to it because of a woman."

"Hard cheese," said Mr Potts.

"And so," hissed the Voice, taking a sinister tone, "if you do not manage an adventure a day, to prove Dangerfield is a match for anyone, I'm afraid I shall have to withdraw my offer of help."

"So be it," said Mr Potts. "I shall deal with the matter myself," and rising before his fingers could reply he dressed in his best open necked lumberjack shirt, yellow cardigan, faded blue corduroy trousers and brown carpet slippers. After checking in the mirror that he looked every inch a gentleman in the Dangerfield mould, he adjusted a filter cigarette at a rakish angle, lit the wrong end, threw it away in disgust and headed for the door.

Three

On his way down to breakfast Mr Potts decided that a Dangerfield approach to this situation could solve all his problems and at the same time show how he was not to be dictated to. As he walked down the thinly carpeted stairs into the familiar aroma of potted plants and mansion polish he imagined the scene as he walked into the kitchen, with a rueful smile on his handsome lips as he exclaimed: "Morning, Mrs Baldwin. Gosh, I had a skinful last night and before you say anything I was going to say I propose to give you enough money to join your sister in Australia. After all, who wants a womaniser and rake like me for a husband. Then with a reckless laugh he would throw himself at his boiled egg and pass the whole thing off with a wave of his toast soldier and a gay laugh.

As he entered the kitchen the pale Sydney leapt from the table and threw his thin arms round the middle of Mr Potts' cardigan.

"Daddy," he cried. " 'Ees my new Daddy."

Mr Potts made a mental note that he must start on the next adventure after breakfast.

"*H*e's," corrected Mrs Harris from the stove as she removed Mr Potts' egg from the pan. "Morning, Mr Potts," she added. "Did you sleep well?"

"Er, yes," lied Mr Potts.

"I didn't," said Mrs Baldwin, rising her hypothyroid eyes gazed lovingly at Mr Potts as he hovered uncertainly in the doorway, still in the grateful grip of his stepson-to-be.

"I haven't slept a wink," she said advancing.

I'm not surprised, thought Mr Potts. Probably can't close her eyelids over those bulging eyes. Then aloud, he said,

"I must have a word with you, Mrs Baldwin."

"Beatrice, she murmured, kissing him tenderly on the cheek, revealing to his sensitive skin a sharp unplucked whisker on her chin.

"Er, Beatrice," he mumbled.

"Come and sit down, you lovebirds," said Mrs Harris, "it's all getting cold."

"What are you goin' to buy me for Christmas, Daddy?" inquired Sydney, immediately getting down to a proper father-son relationship.

"He's not your Daddy yet," admonished Mrs Baldwin, with a wag of her finger.

"But soon, eh?" boomed the Basso Profundo from behind the *News of the World,* which he lowered to reveal his swarthy face which had so recently leered triumphantly at Mr Potts as he consigned him to his fate in the rising waters at Wimbledon.

"And who," continued the unnaturally deep voice, "is going to be the best man?"

"Me, I hope," exclaimed Mr Leopold, in his best Fair Isle sweater from the doorway. "That is," he added anxiously, "unless there is someone else?"

"Er, well, it's early days yet," said Mr Potts, crouching over his egg and feeling like a hunted animal.

"And I have to fill my bottom drawer," said the plump Mrs Baldwin archly.

As if there wasn't enough in there already, thought Mr Potts, as he struck the top of his egg forcefully with the back of his spoon.

"Will you draw a face on mine, Daddy," asked the pale Sydney, indicating his upturned empty eggshell in its cup.

"Don't speak at the table," said Mr Potts, hoping this firm side of his nature would make Sydney regret his enthusiasm.

"Sorry Daddy," said Sydney, lapsing into an unnatural silence that Mr Potts found quite unnerving.

"Isn't he good with children," said Mrs Baldwin admiringly.

It's a diabolical plot, thought Mr Potts, morosely stuffing a toast soldier into his egg with such force the yolk ran over the top.

"He's a guid man," said Mrs Harris.

"The best," said Mr Leopold. "I shall miss him at Ranleigh Road."

"Oh?" said Mr Potts. "Whare are you going?"

"Nowhere," said Mr Leopld, "but I presume you'll be buying a house with your pools win."

"I do not intend leaving 69 Ranleigh Road," said Mr Potts firmly. That'll do it, he thought. "I have become," he continued, "very attached to it."

"I'm so glad," said Mrs Harris, "because I was going to say that you and your wife . . ."

Mr Potts choked on his toast.

" . . . can . . ." continued Mrs Harris, as she topped up the vast flowered teapot, "can have the top floor and we'll clear out the attic and that can be Sydney's playroom."

"Cor, super!" said Sydney. "And if there should be the patter of tiny feet," interjected Mrs Baldwin," we could use it as a nursery."

Mr Potts' inside contracted with horror. Patter of tiny feet! Then, smiling blandly and pretending not to have taken the point, he said casually, "Yes, a dog might be a good idea." "I was not referring to a dog," said Mrs Baldwin with a hint of impatience. "She means a little baby," said the well meaning Mr Leopold, indicating something the size of a banana with his well-manicured hands.

"Oh really," said Mr Potts. Without enthusiasm he picked up the *Sunday Mirror* and disappeared behind it, aware that Mrs Baldwin and Mrs Harris had exchanged meaningful glances and that the opposition must realise it wasn't all going to be plain sailing.

From behind the paper, the centre page of which contained a revealing photo of Brigitte Bardot, who appeared to be giving him a sympathetic smile as she held her bosom up for inspection, he heard Mrs Harris announce.

"Registry?" Then Mrs Baldwin's worrying reply, "I think that'll be quickest and we'll announce it in the *Telegraph*."

I wonder thought Mr Potts, who the next villain is going to be. Only four to deal with, then it was up to P. W. He smiled grimly at Brigitte Bardot and thought what a pity she wasn't working at Pollock Bros.

Against his will, but not wishing to seem churlish for it was by Mrs Harris's invitation, he accompanied the residents of Ranleigh Road to the Red Lion for a Sunday morning aperitif as Mr Leopold described it. Leaving the pale Sydney well wrapped up on the bench seat outside, they entered.

"Don't forget my lemonade, Daddy," he called. Mr Potts pretended not to hear.

"Morning, Signor Baroli, Morning Mrs Harris, Mr Potts," said the red-nosed Bill, from behind the bar, raising a friendly glass.

"Morning all," said Gloria the bosomy barmaid, giving Mr Potts a wink and bending down to wash a glass so he could share with the other regulars a quick view of the valley of desire that existed between her vast bosoms.

"Morning, Gloria," said Mr Potts, remembering how as the oversexed White Sultana, with a male harem, he had ruthlessly left her to her fate in her desert lair. She was another one he must speak to P. W. about. He would insist that all the heroines were desirable in real life or he would ignore their distress signals.

"What'll it be?" said Bill wiping the back of his hand over his frothy moustache.

"Mr Potts, the author," said Mrs Harris grandly, "has become betrothed to Mrs Baldwin, my cousin here, who works in the corsetry department of Pollock Bros."

"Engaged, eh!" said Bill. "This *does* call for a drink and this time it's on yours truly."

"Wonders will never cease," said Mr Leopold. Then quickly, "Campari Dry with a hint of lemon."

"Blimey," said Gloria, with a warm smile, "you randy old devil." And leaning over the bar and causing many regulars to half leave their seats she gave the blushing Mr Potts a smacking kiss on his cheek.

He did not feel the term randy old devil could accurately be applied to him, as he'd only ever taken one girl out for a drink. But no one seemed to take offence, and unless he was mistaken Mrs Baldwin's eyes protruded even more, with an interested gleam.

As they all chattered at once, Bill tugged Mr Potts' sleeve and in a hoarse confidential whisper, inquired, "'Ad a go yet?"

"That is not," said Mr Potts, sternly out of the corner of his mouth, "the sort of question a gentleman would answer."

"Oh, you 'aven't then," said Bill with a hint of disappointment in his voice. Then with a grin he whispered, "I just thought something must 'ave made 'er eyes stand out like that." And with a raucous laugh as Mr Potts winced at the poor taste of his local publican's humour, he buried his nose into yet another tankard of foaming ale, leaving Mr Potts to regret recklessly tossing him a five shilling piece in his recent and more servile role as a driver of a hansom cab.

As the party marched home Mrs Baldwin took Mr Potts' suddenly stiff left arm and pulling herself close and speaking up his nostrils confided that she was not old fashioned in her attitude to the present behaviour pattern of the sexes, and that although it was a drawback, sharing her room with her son, perhaps they might get to know one another better in Mr Potts' room; with her portable radio playing of course, she added, in case inquisitive ears detected sounds of activity foreign to the normal peace and quiet of Ranleigh Road.

Mr Potts adopted a stern and pious expression.

"Beatrice," he said, with all the solemnity that a desperate man could muster, "I think I should tell you that as a devout believer in Zen Buddhism I cannot condone any extramarital thoughts until after the ceremony."

That's fixed her, he thought. Just the sort of thing old P. W. would have said.

"Good heavens," said Mrs Baldwin, "Zen what?"

"Buddhism", said Mr Potts. "Indian religion," he added waving his free arm airily.

"Do I have to be one?" said Mrs Baldwin, anxiously.

"It takes years of training and doing yoga," said Mr Potts, smiling inwardly and congratulating himself on his brainwave. "I can cook fish, if they don't let you eat meat," said the practical Mrs Baldwin. "I do a very good cod sauce." Mr Potts frowned.

"No, we can eat meat," he said hurriedly. "It's just that we, because of our religion, have to treat women as goods and chattels, and of course, European women aren't too keen on that."

"I like a man to be dominant," breathed Mrs Baldwin squeezing his arm, "and as a matter of fact," she confided, "a great uncle of mine on my mother's side served in the Khyber Rifles. He was a very dark man I believe," she said, her eyes protruding earnestly, "so it's possible I have some Indian blood in my veins."

Crikey, thought Mr Potts, to top everything else a touch of the tarbrush! "So we have something in common with you being a Zen," said Mrs Baldwin. Mr Potts walked on in silence thinking how he must get to the typewriter as soon as lunch was over.

On arriving at Ranleigh Road Mr Potts was greeted by an excited Elsie who, waving her oven glove enthusiastically, informed him that a couple had called in answer to his advertisement in the newsagents regarding his car, and he suddenly remembered how fond he was of his battered, red 1932 MG, £125 o.n.o., sitting over a pool of black oil in the garage and how, now, with his winnings he could afford to keep it.

"Did they make an offer?" he asked. "Oh, I didn't let them see it, Mr Potts," said the faithful Elsie. "I just let 'em look through the key 'ole, but I told 'em I couldn't let 'em in without you being there."

"Quite right," said Mr Potts, hanging his hat and coat on the hallstand. "Don't want strangers leaning on that racing bodywork, in case the wings fall off!" said Mr Leopold, then hurriedly as he saw Mr Potts' expression, "Only joking, of course."

"They said they was coming back later," added Elsie, as she disappeared towards the kitchen.

"Lunch overture and beginners, please," called Mrs Harris as she beat the gong into a resounding crescendo, which died away slowly under her skilful hands.

"May I have the pleasure?" boomed Signor Baroli, and proffering his arm he led Mrs Harris into the dining room.

Mr Potts pretended not to notice that Mrs Baldwin had taken his arm and putting his free hand in his pocket, in case

Sydney tried to place his trusting little mitt in it, he entered the dining room determined to break all eating records and retire to his room.

Mr Potts wished he hadn't eaten so quickly. The prolonged burp he had just suffered was an indication that his digestive juices had been taken by surprise and his last Alka Seltzer tablet, with which he had tried to alleviate his condition, had floated fizzlessly on top of the cup of water revealing, on closer inspection, that the compressed cotton wool stopper had fallen to the bottom of the bottle.

Four

Ignoring the rumbling of his uneasy interior, Mr Potts lit a cigarette, making a mental note to remove the nicotine stain on his index finger that had told Holmes where his letter was, and feeling his fingers twitch, he placed the cigarette in the chipped saucer, that served as an ashtray.

"Hello P. W." he said.

"Hello Henry," he typed and the Voice that accompanied the words sounded positively benign. "Sorry if I've been a bit hard on you lately," it continued in time with the keys.

"Oh, that's all right," said Mr Potts. "I'm afraid I've been a bit tense. The Baldwin affair," he added glumly.

"Of course," rattled the keys, "how about a visit to Dangerfield Manor to relax in the grounds?"

"Oh a bit of time off, that's good," said Mr Potts. "Is it a nice day?"

"July the 22nd 1928 was very hot," said the Voice of one who obviously remembered clearly.

"What about my next adversary?" Mr Potts asked keenly. "Think I can handle him?"

"Carl Peterson" typed his fingers, "is no fool." Mr Potts furrowed his brow as he tried to recall who Carl Peterson was.

"You will have no doubt guessed" the Voice continued proudly in time with the activity of the Imperial, "that I have, standing next to me, none other than the late Mr H. C. McNeil, better known by his pen name of Sapper and creator of Bulldog Drummond."

Bulldog Drummond! Mr Potts took a deep drag on his cigarette to calm his nerves. Of course, old Bulldog's famous adversary. Mr Potts narrowed his eyes and tried to recall just how evil Carl Peterson had been. He seemed to remember that Hugh Drummond, despite his enormous physical strength and fists the size of a ham, had nearly had his chips more than once at the hands of this foreign swine.

"I hope," said Mr Potts, "that there is a girl in the affair. A good looking one," he added.

"You will not be disappointed," he typed.

"I've already had a couple of goes at Miss Catchpole of the Bank", reminded Mr Potts. "And Miss Jenkins of the Dancing School was rather overenthusiastic. Of course I realise she was from a primitive tribe but . . ."

"Don't worry," he typed. "This is just your handwriting Henry, and she's relying on you."

"Super," said Mr Potts, "And P.S. P.W. could I have an extra page at thc end this time, so that the heroine has time to thank me properly?"

"Why not?" typed his fingers.

"Thank you," said Mr Potts gratefully.

"This story," tapped the keys, "(plot by H. C. McNeil) is entitled The Last Round But One."

"Ready," said Mr Potts.

In a moment his fleeting fingers had started typing, and the late author's voice confirmed the situation with the words, "and so we find the handsome Captain Gregory Dangerfield in his silk fencing shirt by Bridges of the Burlington Arcade, and white Oxford Bags, by Henshaws, and plimsolls, by Le Sport of Paris, ignoring a face mask and facing a flickering foil, wielded by his faithful valet Masterton, as he keeps in trim on the lawn outside the open French windows of the music room at Dangerfield Manor."

As the sound of the keys died away Mr Potts found himself facing Bill, the red-nosed barman from the Rose and Crown. The froth round his mouth was not by courtesy of the brewery but quite obviously from the effort of keeping his master's deadly blade at bay, for to Mr Potts delight it was obvious he was a master swordsman, as he found himself, hand on hip, toying with his panting menial. Typical of old Arnold, he thought. Keeping his hero in trim. But it was too nice a day to waste and with a quick movement he disarmed his opponent.

"That's it for today, Bill, er, I mean Masterton."

"Yes, Captain," said the grateful Masterton. "You're as good as ever, sir."

"Naturally," said Mr Potts, and sticking his foil into the lawn he casually flicked the end with his finger and as his trusty blade swung to and fro he wandered idly round the beautiful old walled gardens of the manor house smelling the roses.

As the hot 1928 sun beat on his back, and a big cabbage white butterfly zigzagged aimlessly across the beautifully cut green lawns, he wished that the old Imperial was here and that he could occasionally type himself into the struggling world of Henry Potts, to remind himself how lucky he was to be the rich, handsome and permanent Dangerfield. For at this moment he *was* Dangerfield, Lord of the manor, and it was 1928 and no doubt somewhere, in his wide trousers, Leslie Howard was looking at a seagull and sketching the forerunner of the Spitfire. Good old Leslie! In London young Mrs Harris was living in Ranleigh Road rehearsing for the next tour with Mr Harris, and in Sheffield he was — he counted quickly on his fingers — he was three, and living with his dear and not yet departed grandmother. And even Oswald his tortoise was still alive and no doubt hiding in the coal shed.

Mr Potts suddenly had a wild idea. Of course, there must be a telephone at Dangerfield Manor. If only he could remember the number, he could . . . He hurried through the open french windows past a large shining piano with the name Bechstein in gold letters. Must be mine, thought Mr Potts. Wonder who plays? Then he ran into the large hall with the paintings of his good-looking ancestors, then he remembered that they must be all of him, for after all wasn't he Dorian Gray who had visited the Eternal Flame? No wonder he was so good at fencing, and then he spotted it: there on a tray, held by a lifesize wooden carving of a black boy, with staring glass eyes and wearing brightly painted livery, was an old fashioned phone. Picking it up, with his heart pounding in his ears and hoping that P. W. Arnold wasn't about to interrupt, he asked the operator for the number. He heard it ringing. Good Lord, what would he say? Hello Gran, miss you. Sorry you're dead but I'm just passing back in time, through a story and I thought I'd give you a ring. No. He just would hear her voice again, say it was a wrong number and hang up. The ringing stopped and a child's voice said quite clearly.

"Hello."

"Hello," said Mr Potts. "Hello," said the voice.

"Who is this?" said Mr Potts, with a tingling sensation on his neck making the hairs stand out. "Henry Potts," said the small voice.

It's me, thought Mr Potts. I'm talking to me. He was surprised at how polite and grown-up he sounded.

"Gran's out," his voice informed him.

"Oh," said Mr Potts lost for words.

"Goodbye," said the small voice and the receiver at the other end clicked down.

Mr Potts felt quite shaky as he put his receiver down and then tried, as he wandered back towards the garden, to recall answering the phone when he was three to a stranger who never called back. He certainly sounded a nice little boy. Much nicer than Sydney. But then boys were nicer when he was small. He paused by the piano and ran his hands over the polished top. He certainly had some nice furniture. Perhaps Dangerfield played? Something he'd always wanted to do and well worth a try. He sat on the round stool and held out his hands. Did he imagine it or did he feel a familiar tingle? He banged his fingers down on the keys producing a discordant jangle. Damn, thought Mr Potts. What a swizz. Then a thought struck him, perhaps he didn't play by ear.

"He didn't," confirmed P. W. Arnold.

Getting up Mr Potts found some sheet music in the seat of the stool and selecting 'Bye Bye Blues' he placed it on the rest and tried again. To his delight he heard P. W. Arnold's voice exclaim in his ear, "With the expertise of Jelly Roll Morton in his heyday, Dangerfield allowed his slim fingers to fly over the keys as he sang to himself in his own inimitable style, the style that had sent shivers down the spines of some of the most beautiful women in Europe and had earned the envy of Fred Astaire, who is said to have copied his style with great success.

Gosh so I'm that good, thought Mr Potts. And I sing too. He banged his fingers down again among the keys and to his delight his hands played with the expertise with which he typed his adventures. In a moment he had thrown back his head and was accompanying himself with Dangerfield's attractive husky voice. "Not unlike that of the late Whispering Jack Smith," shouted the voice of his creator.

How Mr Potts wished the blondish brunette from the Post Office could be there to swoon on the expensive carpet; but he was alone.

But what was that he could hear? Yes, it was P. W. Arnold shouting something. But what? Pausing in the middle of a tricky arpeggio Mr Potts strained his keen Dangerfield ears as the last notes died away. " . . . hadn't heard" shouted the Voice, "the sound of the small dirigible engines and the almost noiseless step behind him."

Mr Potts tried to turn, but too late. An arm like a vice closed on his neck and a compelling, slightly foreign voice whispered sinisterly in his ear.

"One move," it said, "and I will break your neck." Mr Pott's heart missed a beat.

"It was not often," said the surprised voice of the late P. W. Arnold, "that Captain Gregory Dangerfield, perhaps the world's most perfect fighting machine, was taken off guard! But by who?"

By who indeed? thought Mr Potts. Perhaps a neighbour who didn't like Whispering Jack Smith? Surely "Bye Bye Blues" was not to be his epitaph?

"It was," said P. W. Arnold, tensely and speaking quickly, "none other than Carl Peterson, who, having kidnapped the beautiful Elizabeth Milton-Essex-Wake-Wickham, daughter of Sir Basil Fortescue-Essex-Wake-Wickham (the arms magnate), had been foiled in his plot to hold her to ransom by none other than Bulldog Drummond. He, although drugged by the poisonous pill placed in his pint pewter pot as he assuaged his thirst in the Thrush & Thistle at Thruxstead, managed to drive his Bentley to Peterson's hideout at Haddenham, free the girl, who is at this moment at the wheel of Drummond's Bentley, with Drummond dead to the world in the dicky. She is driving to the house of her father's fearless friend Captain Gregory Dangerfield, who at this moment is held in a Herculean head lock by the evil Peterson as he awaits her arrival having accurately assessed her intentions. He arrived before her in his private airship, the twin 80 h.p. Maybach engines of which drone faintly as it hovers above Dangerfield Manor supporting the observation car on the end of its cable outside the window of the music room, through which the arch villain silently stopped but a moment ago."

Mr Potts' neck was quite stiff and there was a buzzing in his ears by the time the late author had finished. So that's what had happened. Well obviously some comment was called for. After all, it was not often that this magnificent fighting machine, that played the piano so well, was taken by surprise. Then he remembered a sure-fire remark that always took the villains off their guard. "Look out behind you," he wheezed.

The effect was more dramatic that he had hoped for. His handsome head was beaten twice sharply on the top of the piano, causing him to blink his eyes rapidly to refocus them and gaze anxiously at the piano to make sure it wasn't marked.

"Shush," said Peterson, "I am listening."

Mr Potts suddenly realised he could see his assailant's reflection in the polished woodwork. His heart missed a beat for it was his friendly bank manager, that had been so accommodating, who was now raising something above his head preparatory to parting Dangerfield's hair with it.

"Seizing his chance," said the urgent Voice of P. W. Arnold, "Dangerfield, whose reflexes are reputed to be faster than those of the Brazilian fly-eating snapdragon, shot his lean right elbow like a piston into the pit of his adversary's plexus." A gasp of agony greeted Mr Potts' ears as his lean elbow flew back and the grip on his neck relaxed.

"Whipping round with the speed of a blind Indian beggar hearing a rupee drop," said the author, "Dangerfield sprang."

Mr Potts whipped round with great alacrity but forgot to rise from the piano stool which, being adjustable, continued to spin round causing him to ascend sharply above the level of the keyboard, until it came to a sudden halt propelling his gyrating body off at a tangent.

"Throwing his cat-like body aside," said the accommodating P. W. Arnold, "to escape the bullet that Peterson fired from his Luxor 33, he flung himself behind the Louis IV chaise longue (on which he had shared a moment of magic with the nubile Catherine Von Klutz but 24 hours previously, after rescuing her from the occult circle who were to sacrifice her to Satan in a disused synagogue at Sydenham. What unmentionable rites he'd had to endure disguised as the god Pan, whose birthday it was, before bounding to his Bugatti and fleeing to freedom with a fainting female, will remain seared indelibly on his mind forever)."

It's all go, thought Mr Potts, as he tried to clear his spinning head. What a pity the story hadn't started yesterday. Another shot which splintered the leg of his valuable chaise longue reminded him of his predicament.

"With his jaw jutting dangerously," said the encouraging voice of the late P. W. Arnold, "Dangerfield picked up the chaise longue and threw it at his adversary." Mr Potts felt the familiar flow of adrenalin that always came in times of stress, and reminding himself that he mustn't let his new overdraft facilities sway his judgement, he gripped the chaise longue and threw it at his adversary, who fired twice wildly as he fell to the accompaniment of twanging wires as both bullets hit the piano. The swine, thought Mr Potts, my best Bechstein, and — horror of horrors — the valuable chaise longue of happy memories had lost a leg. The suddenly houseproud Mr Potts made a mental note not to use the leg to beat the bank manager to death in case he couldn't get the stain out of the carpet.

"Dangerfield bounded across the hall towards the gun room," said the excited voice of P. W. Arnold. "He heard the roar of a car in the driveway and his keen ears recognised immediately that it was a blown Black Label Bentley with enlarged inlet valves with a 7.5 to 1 compression, and he knew that Peterson's quarry had arrived."

"Masterton," he called sternly, as he peered at a choice of doorways searching for the gun room. "Masterton! Where are you?" He clicked his tongue in annoyance. Here he was, fighting for his life, while his trusted valet was no doubt having a crafty smoke in the Karzi. He hurriedly corrected himself — "I mean the loo." He mustn't forget where he was.

"Spotting," said the voice in his ear, "the green door with the brass plate on which are clearly engraved the words Gun Room, he entered."

Mr Potts ignored the sarcastic tone and rushed into the room. For a second the sight took his breath away. He took in the animal heads on the walls. Was he, Henry Potts the animal lover, responsible for removing this wild life from one happy hunting ground and sending it to another? "Yes," snapped the voice of Dangerfield's creator, "he was. And you'll be joining them if you don't look sharp."

Mr Potts leapt for the row of guns that completely covered one wall. Things must be bad, he thought for old P. W. to break into the story line. He must remember he was Dangerfield the hunter. Pulling down the biggest gun he could see, he staggered back under its weight and peered anxiously out towards the hall.

"Taking," said the voice of the late P. W. Arnold, "his favourite elephant gun, by Butt Bros, of Rangoon and given to him by the much scented maharajah of Jaipong in return for Dangerfield's unerring accuracy in shooting off the head of the black baboon-headed viper that had slithered silently up the sleeping Maharajah's silk pyjamas on to appear from the aperture beneath his pyjama cord, hissing sibilantly, (the decapitation of which had been witnessed and misinterpreted by her Serene Highness Princess Popodom, formerly Doris Windybanks the All England ice skater, who had after a cry of dismay lapsed into a deep coma for the rest of the rainy season)."

Mr Potts anxiously chewed his lip; how could he be expected to hear the prowling Peterson when old P. W. went on like that? Where was he and where had the car gone? As though to answer both questions, a shot shattered the glass eye of a tiger's head nearby and as Mr Potts flattened himself next to a french window he heard the sound of the car approaching again. Gazing out he saw to his horror that it was travelling across his well cut lawn and over the flower-beds. His beautiful garden! Why couldn't all this have happened at Peterson's place.

Then, out of the corner of his eye, he spotted a figure crossing the doorway, above which was the head of a stuffed rhino, and raising the vast gun to his right shoulder he squinted keenly between the twin barrels and pulled the trigger. The effect was dramatic. The rhino's head, together with most of the wall above the doorway, disappeared.

The recoil threw the startled Mr Potts back against a row of shelves, which collapsed causing a large green box to fall on his head. Its surprise arrival made his already twitching trigger finger tighten and as the second barrel blasted and a large hole appeared in the wall next to the door Mr Potts slumped, deafened, to the floor and through the hole in the wall he observed the pale figure of his shaken adversary clutching a revolver.

Mr Potts' overtaxed nerves gave an almost audible twang.

"It was Peterson seeking revenge," confirmed the tense voice of the late P. W. Arnold, "for his narrow escape from the fearsome firepower that Dangerfield had used with such deadly effect." Mr Potts gazed transfixed as the pale-looking arch villain shakily raised his gun.

"Goodbye," said Peterson hoarsely.

"Goodbye," said Mr Potts weakly. Then to his surprise it was Peterson's turn to gaze transfixed.

Mr Potts followed his gaze. What was that greenish little pineapple-looking object rolling across the floor? Then he realised that it had come from the upturned green box that lay surrounded by more green pineapples at his feet. Even though it was upside down, he could clearly read the words — Mills Bombs — on the side.

"Realising," said the faint voice of P. W. Arnold in Mr Potts' still ringing ears, "that Dangerfield was prepared to blow himself up to rid the world of this arch villain, Peterson turned tail and ran for it."

Mr Potts sat frozen with horror. He tried to move but his muscles felt like perished rubber bands.

"If Dangerfield," continued the late author, "was to save his skin, there was only one recourse. He must throw himself head first out of the nearest window."

With a tremendous effort Mr Potts staggered to his feet unable to take his eyes off the bomb which had stopped in the doorway. Dangerfield's strength seemed to have deserted him. How was he going to get to the window, never mind throw himself through it? As though in answer, the bomb exploded and Mr Potts felt himself picked up by an invisible hand which propelled him head first and seemingly painlessly through the window and into the garden. There he lay, with the thunderous explosion ringing in his ears and as he gazed at the blue sky, he wondered if there would be anything left of his ancestral home before the day was out.

The roar of the approaching car made him roll to one side and as it came to a halt he saw a beautiful blonde girl, wearing a short skirt and long beads. First time I've seen her, thought Mr Potts. Must be a real Twenties heroine.

"Quick Gregoreah Dharling," she said as she leapt athletically out of the car. "Aim in the most awful trouble."

"It was," said P. W. Arnold, "the beautiful, society playgirl and daring aeronaut, Elisabeth Milton-Essex-Wake-Wickham." Who else, thought Mr Potts, noting as she knelt by him that her brief underwear matched her limpid blue eyes.

Then, in a commanding Dangerfield voice, he said, "Quick, help me to my feet."

"What about poor Hugh?" she said. "He's in the dickeh of the Bentleh."

"I'll get him," said Mr Potts.

As Miss Wickham helped him to his feet a whirring sound caught his ear and glancing up he saw something like a small, open-topped telephone box, containing his fist-shaking adversary, rising above the roof of Dangerfield Manor. Above this, suspended in the sky, was a small cigar-shaped airship with a gondola slung under it. Peterson's Dirigible, thought Mr Potts, and he's quitting. Not surprising after dealing with a madman like Dangerfield.

Staggering to the back of the car. he found himself gazing into the unmistakeably pugnacious face of the huge man, in the rough Harris tweed sports jacket, who was slumped unconscious in the seat.

"Yes, it was Bulldog Drummond," said the voice of P. W. Arnold, "and only a man with the strength of Man Mountain Dean could have lifted his vast inert body with such ease and carried him into the house."

With a tremendous effort Mr Potts managed to drag Drummond out of the car. Old Hugh, he thought, is definitely overweight, but then he does drink a pint of beer on every other page! And then it struck him that he'd never seen Drummond before either. Not even in the Rose & Crown. So this was really Bulldog Drummond and Miss Wake-Wickham really was a Twenties heroine.

"Let me 'elp you, Captain."

Mr Potts paused and turned. Thank heavens. It was Masterton.

"'Ad a bit of a foray I see, Captain," he said, grabbing the inert Drummond's legs.

"Yes," said Mr Potts. "This is Captain Hugh Drummond."

"Yes sir. I knew his batman . . ." said Masterton. "We was both at Vimy Ridge, when you wiped out that German machine gun. When they give you your second V.C., Captain. Don't you remember?"

"Oh, that V.C.," said Mr Potts. "Of course." And puffing and panting they dragged the dead-to-the-world Drummond into the hall, which Mr Potts noted to his dismay was much larger since the bomb had exploded.

"In heh," said Miss Wickham, holding open a door.

As Mr Potts entered the room dragging Drummond by the shoulders, he gazed in admiration and relief at the untouched elegance of it all. What a smashing private lounge, he thought, as he dropped the inert body and gazed admiringly at the beautiful wing-backed chairs and big sofas resting on a richly embroidered Indian carpet. His admiring gaze took in the expensive looking cocktail cabinet, the glass cases with china figures on their shelves and the vast fireplace with lots of impressive looking invitations on the mantelpiece. He felt, recalling his sparse room at Ranleigh Road, that this was how he should always live and he would have his man tidy up the mess in the hall and the music room as soon as possible.

He was brought out of his admiring reverie by Miss Wickham, patting Drummond's unresponsive cheek and calling, "Hugh Dahling, wake up. Plears for my sake."

"What the hell?" murmured a deep voice. "Where am I? I'll get him, the swine."

Good, thought Mr Potts, old Hugh was coming out of his drugged sleep and would soon be ready to pub crawl his way home. Kneeling down by the prostrate but now stirring form and patting it on the Harris tweed shoulder, he said in his best gritty Dangerfield voice, "Hello Hugh old lad." His friends always called him "Hugh". "I don't think we've met."

He was quite unprepared for the violent punch he received between the eyes as the vast figure of Drummond rose from its resting place with a bellow of anger.

"I'll break every bone in your body," cried the staring eyed figure as it staggered to its feet.

"'E's still a bit groggy," exclaimed Masterton as he helped the dazed Mr Potts to his feet.

"Hugh Dahling!" screamed Miss Wickham, "calm down."

"Got to get out," muttered Drummond, and to Mr Potts' horror Mr H. C. McNeil's dogged hero, who never knew when he was beaten, suddenly thrust a size 13 shoe through the cocktail cabinet, causing the broken bottles to disgorge their multicoloured contents on to the carpet. Never get that out, thought Mr Potts miserably, as he tenderly held his nose and watched a fist, the size of a ham, swing back and punch a hole through the case with the china figures. Then, staggering drunkenly, Drummond tripped over a coffee table and tore down the curtains in an effort to save himself. Knocking two pictures off the wall he threw himself, head first, through the door tearing it off its hinges and disappeared into the hall with the triumphant yell of, "My God, chaps, we've made it!"

Mr Henry Potts felt glad Drummond was on his side, but disappointed that Dangerfield Manor had gone down in value so rapidly since his arrival.

"Well, Miss Wickham," he said, baring his teeth and allowing a light smile to flicker in his steely blue eyes. "It's all over."

"Gregoreh Dharling," she cried and flinging her arms around his neck, she said, "I'll do anythingh you want to show har grateful I am."

"Dangerfield," said the Voice of the late P. W. Arnold, "felt her small perfumed breasts thrust sharply against his silk shirt. Her hair cascaded over her limpid blue eyes that turned into a vortex of desire as they gazed into his."

Thank goodness, thought Mr Potts, that he had asked P. W. for an extra page, for there was something he couldn't wait to do.

A few moments later, in the Music Room, Mr Potts had handed the surprised Miss Wickham the dust pan and brush that Masterton had produced, and as she gratefully worked to clear up the mess, assisted by Masterton with a broom, Mr Potts sat down at the piano and placing his Jelly Roll Morton fingers on the keyboard, he allowed his husky Whispering Jack Smith voice to sing "Bye Bye Blues" despite the occasional discord, caused by the bullets of the departed Peterson, who had mistakenly bearded the lion in his den.

He found he had time to get half-way through a hectic rendering of "Happy Feet" before he heard the amused voice of the late P. W. Arnold.

And so as Miss Wickham showed her gratitude, we say farewell for the moment to the bravest, handsomest, most talented man in the world, Captain Gregory Dangerfield."

Five

It wasn't until the enthusiastic Mr Potts found that he was suddenly singing in an offkey voice and playing on the typewriter keys that he realised that his musical career was over for the time being, and that he was once again at Ranleigh Road. Mr Potts was in the middle of enjoying a cup of tea and recapturing his recent adventure in the written word when Elsie announced that the couple had come back to look at his car.

Mr Potts followed her down the stairs and stopped halfway down the last flight with a gasp of surprise. For there, standing in the hall, holding a peaked cap in his hand and wearing a checked sports jacket, was quite unmistakeable Bulldog Drummond. And, by his side, the recently unrequited Miss Wickham, wearing a duffel coat. Mr Potts' mind raced. Was he still upstairs? And had he just typed them into his life or what?

In a hoarse Cockney voice Bulldog spoke. "'Ello," he said, "we come about the advert."

"We was lookin' for an MG," confirmed Miss Wickham, "and we was told to come back."

Mr Potts realised that P. W. Arnold had, after all, taken his supporting cast from real life while he himself was out.

"Oh, hello," he said. "I'm Henry Potts, the author, who has an MG for sale. It's in the garage. I'll show you." A moment later he was opening the creaking doors of the garage to reveal his battered pride and joy. He looked at the would-be purchaser, waiting for his exclamation of surprise and delight.

The couple stared at the battered bodywork in silence, and Mr Potts coughed to hide the sound of the dripping oil. The couple then exchanged glances and Mr Potts knew how they felt, for to find an almost original 1932 MG was almost unheard of.

"Well?" he said with a smile of pride. "I am open to offers."

"Then sling it on the rubbish dump," said Bulldog gruffly, turning to go.

"Now look here," said Mr Potts.

"Wot a load of old rubbish," said Miss Wickham, turning her nose in the air.

As they walked to the gate Mr Harris breathed a sight of relief. Thank goodness he'd played the piano instead of giving Miss Wickham a magical moment on the battered chaise longue.

On returning indoors he was confronted by a bulging eyed Mrs Baldwin, a sad-faced Sydney, a hopeful Mrs Harris and a long-faced Mr Leopold. It was obvious to Mr Potts that the news was about to have a mixed reception.

"They decided it was too expensive," said Mr Potts.

"I like that car, so I'm glad," said Mr Leopold. "It's really you."

"Bother," said Mrs Baldwin.

"Pity," said Mrs Harris.

"Good," said Sydney. "I 'aven't 'ad a ride yet."

"Haven't and had," said Mrs Harris.

"I do hope you'll get a closed in one soon," said Mrs Baldwin. "It's too cold for sports cars."

"Well, we won't take it out until the summer then," said Mr Potts heading for the stairs.

"Will you be in for dinner?" said Mrs Harris. "Mrs Baldwin thought perhaps you might be taking her out."

"Taking her out," said Mr Potts.

"You know, to discuss things," sniffed Mrs Baldwin, smiling archly.

Mr Potts was about to say "I'm afraid I'm not well and must go to bed" when an idea struck him. "What a good idea," he said. "I know a nice little cafe near Windsor where we can talk about our honeymoon."

"Our honeymoon," breathed Mrs Baldwin ecstatically closing her eyes and giving Mr Potts a momentary respite from her stare. Then opening them as the thought struck her and she said, "But how on earth are we going to get to Windsor? It's miles away. Shouldn't we go somewhere nearer?"

"By car," said Mr Potts cheerfully. "Better wrap up."

"But . . . " said Mrs Baldwin anxiously.

"Great fun," said Mr Potts. "You'll enjoy it."

Before she could protest further he had fled up the stairs with his face to the wall to hide the wide grin that her dismayed face had produced.

"This will convince her," said Mr Potts to his reflection in the washstand mirror, "that the sporty Henry Potts is altogether too robust a character to be married." His heavily mufflered reflection gazed back revealing only his spectacles under the peak of his racing cap. The rest of his face was hidden under the long scarf, wrapped twice round and tied in a huge knot at the back. Adjusting his cap with his gauntletted hands and making sure the belt of his long raincoat was secure, he went downstairs and knocked at Mrs Baldwin's door.

"Come in," she called.

Mr Potts entered and Mrs Baldwin gave a gasp of surprise at the sight of him.

"Ready?" said Mr Potts' muffled voice.

"Can I come?" said Sydney.

"I'm afraid it's only a two seater," said Mr Potts.

"Couldn't we go somewhere local?" inquired Mrs Baldwin anxiously as she buttoned up her best coat and pinned on her head a small blue hat. "Windsor is so far away."

"Not the way I drive," said Mr Potts significantly clapping his gauntletted hands together and giving a muffled laugh.

"You're not going to drive too fast, I hope," said Mrs Baldwin pulling on a pair of woollen gloves and picking up her handbag.

"Don't worry, I'll keep it under a hundred," said Mr Potts truthfully.

Suddenly he felt like Kenneth More in Genevieve, a sporty, reckless car fanatic, just the sort of person Mrs Baldwin would hate to be married to he hoped.

"Do be careful," said Mrs Harris, as she accompanied them to the front door.

"Don't worry, I'm fully insured," said Mr Potts.

"Goodbye," boomed Signor Baroli, appearing on the stairway in a faded, offwhite suit and sporting a large red carnation.

"I wish we were coming too, but Mrs Harris and I are going to leesen to the great Benjamino Gigli."

"I thought he was dead," said Mrs Baldwin.

"On a wax cylinder recording," said Mrs Harris. "The late Mr Harris left a wonderful collection, mostly of himself of course but one or two of the other great artists."

So that's why Baroli was wearing his concert suit, thought Mr Potts. For a concert in Mrs Harris's private lounge. Old P. W. wouldn't be too pleased about that, and come to think of it, neither would the late Mr Harris. He glanced at the portrait hanging near the barometer. He noticed that a deep depression was indicated, apparently shared by Mr Harris, who seemed to be shouting a silent insult at his white-clad rival.

Leaving the Peyton Place of Streatham, Mr Potts ushered the reluctant Mrs Baldwin out into the cold night air.

"Oh dear," said Mrs Baldwin, as she forced herself into the tiny seat. "There isn't much room."

"You'll soon get used to it," said Mr Potts. "Just hang on to the crash bar."

"What about the hood?" asked Mrs Baldwin. "Can't we have the hood up?"

"Unfortunately," lied Mr Potts as he put the key in the ignition, "it's broken." And pressing the starter, he listened keenly to the familiar judding roar of the 8 h.p. that was waiting to unleash the red projectile into the night.

"It's very loud," shouted Mrs Baldwin hesitantly. Mr Potts nodded.

"Racing engine," he shouted above the clatter. "You'll need these," he added, handing Mrs Baldwin a battered pair of goggles. "Oh dear, will I?" gasped Mrs Baldwin. Mr Potts nodded, and taking them from her, he pulled back the elastic and snapped it down behind her blue hat and pulled them over her eyes.

After a number of attempts he managed to select the elusive reverse gear and, enveloped in a cloud of smoke from the rattling exhaust, backed out of the garage with Mrs Baldwin clutching grimly on to the crash bar with both hands.

"Hold on to your hat," shouted Mr Potts from behind his scarf, and as Mrs Baldwin took him literally, he revved up the protesting engine and noisily selecting first, after hopping like a demented kangaroo, the Red MG disappeared down Ranleigh Road, to the accompaniment of many barking dogs and the envious gaze of Sydney from an upstairs window.

Once on the open road, Mrs Baldwin seemed to relax.

"You're a very good driver," she shouted, turning her goggled face towards Mr Potts' stern profile as he wrestled with the play in the large string-bound wooden steering wheel. Mr Potts nodded and peered ahead into the slight mist that his faint headlights found difficulty in penetrating. He glanced at the wavering speedometer, which alternated between 50 and 80. Doing nearly 60, he thought. He swerved suddenly as a Green Line bus swept past and wrestled with the wheel as the small car swayed about in its wake.

"Road hog," shouted Mrs Baldwin, shaking her fist as it disappeared into the mist.

A worried frown appeared under the peak of Mr Potts' cap. Surely Mrs Baldwin wasn't enjoying the drive? He suddenly spun the wheel wildly as a sharp curve appeared. The tyres squealed and the back started to slide, sending his heart into his mouth.

"Yippee!" shouted the goggled Mrs Baldwin. "You're a real Fangio." I wonder how old she really is, thought Mr Potts, as he managed to get the nose pointing in a straight line again. The mist parted to reveal a stretch of open road.

"Give it the gun," shouted Mrs Baldwin. Perhaps her hypothyroid's gone mad, thought Mr Potts. She certainly didn't seem to be suffering from the cold, his hands had gone numb and the tip of his exposed nose had most probably got frostbite.

Mr Potts pushed the accelerator down, but if anything the car slowed slightly. Damn, clutch slipping again, thought Mr Potts. He must be mad driving at 60. The whole car might fall apart and the goggled Mrs Baldwin was actually bouncing up and down in her seat urging him to go faster.

Mr Potts was more than relieved to arrive at Windsor, where he parked outside a small fish and chip restaurant, which had been the most unsuitable place he could think of.

They entered and his glasses immediately steamed over in the hot atmosphere. On taking them off he observed Mrs Baldwin wandering round helplessly bumping into tables. Hurriedly he took her by the arm and removed her goggles, to reveal her eyes popping with enthusiasm.

"I did enjoy that," she said. "On no account must you sell that car, Henry."

The frozen Mr Potts sat stiffly at the table, while Mrs Baldwin devoured what was apparently her favourite dish, plaice and chips with plenty of vinegar.

"Perhaps," said Mrs Baldwin, as she poured more vinegar on her second helping of chips, "a motoring holiday in Scotland would be an ideal honeymoon idea, and perhaps if I took my test I could have a drive."

Mr Potts nodded glumly, thinking he could, as a last resort, fix the brakes, remove his St Christopher from the key ring, and send her off on a tortuous mountain road.

Then aloud, he said, "Yes, perhaps, but of course that's quite a long way away."

"Ah, of course," said Mrs Baldwin, "we must fix the wedding date. What about next month? I think that just about gives us enough time."

Mr Potts swallowed a very hot chip and calmed his coughing fit with a long drink of tea.

"We have," he gasped, "to be sure we are compatible."

"But," said Mrs Baldwin, leaning forward conspiratorily, "I thought that, you being a Zen weren't allowed to, you know . . . to do it before the wedding night."

"I mean mentally compatible," whispered Mr Potts, hoping this intimate part of their discussion was not being overheard by the staring Indian at the next table.

"Well, I admire your intellectual mind," said Mrs Baldwin, ticking off Mr Potts' good points on her fingers. "And I never imagined I'd like driving in a sports car, but you've changed all that."

Mr Potts ground his teeth in annoyance.

"Sydney adores you," she said, "and of course he needs a daddy." Mr Potts nodded as she hammered the final nails in his coffin.

"And it's time I settled down," she said. "Of course, I've had other offers, what girl hasn't," she fluttered her eyelids and took a noisy sip of tea. "In fact," she added archly, "there was one gentleman that come . . . came," she corrected herself, "into Pollocks to buy some corsetry for his girlfriend who made quite a pass at me."

Mr Potts felt like saying "and if his guide dog hadn't dragged him away he could have been in the same boat", but aloud he said: "I'm sure there have been others. But, of course, if anything happened, er . . . that is to say, if for any reason we were *not* to wed, there would," he said encouragingly, "be others again. After all, there are not many women like you who are single."

"No," said Mrs Baldwin, "that's true. But I've made up my mind, you see," she said earnestly, "with my heart being weak, although the doctors say it's wind, it would be a great comfort for me to know that Sydney had a proper daddy to bring him up."

The words, "the doctors say it's only wind," flashed like neon lights in Mr Potts' brain. Did that mean his fear of telling her that it was a mistake had been groundless, and that she would not after all have fallen down clutching her chest, leaving Sydney an orphan? Blast. Now he was committed. With witnesses, and apart from the obvious defects there was probably nothing wrong with Mrs Baldwin at all.

Mr Potts revised his earlier plan. If they did marry he would fix the brakes, throw away his St Christopher, and go for a drive himself. Calling for the bill and turning down Mrs Baldwin's offer to share it, he headed for the car and started to erect the hood.

"I thought it was broken?" said Mrs Baldwin, who like a

trained Pekinese, was already wearing her goggles.

"Oh, it'll be all right if we drive slowly," said Mr Potts.

"Do we have to?" said Mrs Baldwin.

"Only for Sydney's sake," said Mr Potts, climbing stiffly in.

As they drove slowly back to Ranleigh Road, with Mrs Baldwin chattering about how she hoped he didn't mind cold feet, as her circulation wasn't too good, Mr Potts resolved to start his third adventure as soon as possible. For when he had completed his heroic tasks as Dangerfield then he could expect the late P. W. Arnold to get him out of the tightest spot of his life.

It wasn't until Mr Potts had locked the door of his room and plugged in his electric kettle that he realised he had an excruciating tooth ache in the back molar which had reacted so violently to the silver paper he'd eaten with his chocolate last Saturday. Brought on, thought Mr Potts, by the cold night air from which his frozen extremities were only slowly recovering.

As he waited for the kettle to boil he tried the Gerba method of deep concentration, used so successfully by Dangerfield, but after a few minutes he gave up and crept downstairs. Perhaps a spot of Mrs Harris's whisky would help. The hall was in darkness, but through the coloured glass panels of the front door the street lights threw a faint glow. Stealthily crossing the shadow of the aspidistra plant, Mr Potts paused outside the slightly open door of Mrs Harris's darkened living room. He was just about to enter when to his surprise he heard Mrs Harris speak in a low voice.

"It is not easy being a woman alone," she said.

Mr Potts' heart missed a beat. Mrs Harris was still up and he had nearly walked into her room, where she was no doubt holding communion with the late Mr Harris's portrait.

"I feel so close to you," intoned the invincible Mrs Harris.

Mr Potts imagined the scene. The vast Mrs Harris kneeling in front of the famous baritone's portrait, a flickering candle, as she sought spiritual guidance from her departed husband.

"Kees me again," murmured a familiar voice in a sotto basso profundo. Even with it's muted tone Mr Potts distinctly heard the tinkle of vibrating glasses in the cocktail cabinet. Mr Potts tried to tear himself away, but his legs refused to move. "This is madness," breathed Mrs Harris. "We must stop before it's too late."

And Mr Potts' keen ears detected the rustling of bombazine and deep breathing, followed by the twang of a spring in the old chaise longue. Mr Potts wondered whether the sounds indicated it was already too late, when the glasses tinkled again.

"I geeve you my heart, my dearest one. Everytheeng I have have ees yours. Thees of course includes my post office account."

"Oh Signor Alberto," breathed Mrs Harris. "Pleeze say you weel give me your hand," mumbled Signor Baroli.

Mr Potts, tooth ache forgotten, listened hypnotised as more rustling and deep breathing indicated that it was not only Mrs Harris's hand that was in jeopardy. Poor Mrs Harris, thought Mr Potts, alone all these years, and as a result susceptible to the advances of this former close friend of her husband's. What if in a weak moment she gave in? How she would regret it. Mr Potts steeled himself: there was only one way to prevent her making a hasty decision. It was up to him.

He took a deep breath and backed away to the bottom of the stairs. Then, whistling loudly, he marched purposefully across the tiled floor and knocked firmly on the door. A "Mama Mia" followed by a crash indicating a fall, followed by a strangled "Just a moment please" from Mrs Harris, followed by a discord from the piano, indicated to Mr Potts that he should have whistled louder. The light went on and the door closed with a bang.

Mr Potts wondered whether to run for it and hope they'd never know who knocked, but before he could move, the door opened again revealing half of Mrs Harris's flushed face. But being the old trooper she was, her voice betrayed not a tremor as she spoke.

"Oh it's you, Mr Potts," she said. "I was just having a nap, er before I went to bed."

"Sorry to bother you, Mrs Harris," said Mr Potts, pretending not to notice the tangled remains of Signor Baroli's carnation hanging off a hairpin at the side of her head. "But I have the most awful tooth ache." Mr Potts pointed to the side of his jaw and as he did so he became aware that his tooth ache had completely disappeared and he continued feigning severe pain. "I thought that a spot of whisky . . ."

"Oh you poor thing," said Mrs Harris, as she pushed back her straying locks. "Now you just wait there."

The door closed and Mr Potts applied an ear to one of the panels.

"Where are you?" whispered Mrs Harris.

"Behind the curtain," came the muffled reply.

"It was Mr Potts with a tooth ache," whispered Mrs Harris. "He's outside the door."

Mr Potts imagined Signor Baroli thankfully dabbing his forehead below the hairline and breathing a sigh of relief as he made his entrance from between the velvet curtains. A clink of bottles made Mr Potts take a step back and fixing a painridden look on his face, he held out a grateful hand as Mrs Harris's arm appeared round the door with a whisky bottle.

"Take it to your room" said Mrs Harris.

"Thank you," said Mr Potts, "and I'm sorry to have troubled you."

"Not at all," said Mrs Harris, half her face peering through the narrow gap. "Off to bed with you now."

Mr Potts felt Mrs Harris's anxious eye boring into his back as he recrossed the hall and headed up the stairs. Well, he thought, at least she had been saved for the moment. But how much longer could she hold out against the amorous Signor Baroli's advances.

Mr Potts found that his kettle had boiled dry and the plug had sprung out. With a frown of annoyance he picked it up and took it down to the bathroom, taking care to walk on tiptoe. He wouldn't like Mrs Harris to think he was coming down to her room again. He paused outside the bathroom door, all was quiet. Opening the door Mr Potts entered and then stopped in his tracks as the picture he saw printed itself indelibly in his mind.

Mrs Baldwin, wearing curlers and reading a book, was sitting on the lavatory with her Directoires round her ankles. Mrs Baldwin's eyes conveyed that she was just as surprised as Mr Potts. Then opening her mouth, she uttered a piercing scream causing Mr Potts to do a backward standing jump out of the door, which he somehow managed to shut on the way. The moment of silence that followed allowed Mr Potts to distinctly hear the crash of breaking glass from Mrs Harris's private lounge. Gingerly he tapped on the door. "So sorry," he said. "I do hope you're all right." He paused, but as no reply came, he continued. "You see I came to fill my kettle." He held it up, then realising that Mrs Baldwin couldn't see it, lowered it again.

"I thought I'd locked the door," whispered the distraught Mrs Baldwin. "Ah," said Mr Potts. There was a pause and feeling some further remark was called for, he whispered. "Sleep well, Mrs Baldwin." With the sound of the cistern flushing in the distance, he thankfully entered his room and closed the door.

Mr Potts poured out half a cupful of whisky and, toasting his pale reflection in the washstand mirror, took a large gulp. His pale reflection obviously didn't like it and pulled a wry face, but Mr Potts threw back his head and determinedly finished it to the last drop. What a shock that had been. He shuddered as the picture flashed up on his mental cinema screen. Then he reminded himself that when they were married it would probably be an everyday occurrence. No doubt Elizabeth Taylor often sat on the loo reading a paper, but somehow Mrs Baldwin with her Directoires round her ankles did not have the same magic.

Six

"P. W. you've got to help me," said Mr Potts, addressing the ceiling. No sooner had he spoken than his arms straightened out and he felt himself drawn across the room to the old Imperial typewriter. He hardly had time to sit before his fingers were busying themselves among the faded keys.

"It's got to stop," he typed and the late author's irate voice in his ear emphasised the urgency of the message.

"What has?" said Mr Potts.

"This Baroli fellow and Mrs Harris. Only after her money and she has little enough," hammered the keys. "If I was alive," he continued, "I'd give him a damned good hiding . . ."

Mr Potts felt quite alarmed by the anger in the late author's voice. The old boy will give himself a heart attack if he's not careful, thought Mr Potts. Then he realised that a heart attack on the other side wasn't too serious a fate.

"I agree, P. W.," he said in a stern voice. "If there is anything I can do to help just say the word."

"I mean, what does she see in him?" he typed.

"Lord knows," said Mr Potts. "Apart from his awful singing voice he's just a tall fat man with too much hair."

Mr Potts gazed morosely at his reflection and patted his thin untidy hair into place.

"Women seem to like a lot of hair," he rejoined, "Mine's always been thin."

"We are not concerned with your hair, Henry," he typed.

"Sorry," said Mr Potts.

"Now," clattered the keys, "he must have an Achilles heel somewhere."

"You mean built-up shoes," said Mr Potts keenly, as he

tried to recall the Basso Profundo's footwear.

"Blast you," he typed and the author's tone confirmed he was losing patience. "I mean," continued the keys, "he must have a chink in his armour, a weak point."

"Vanity," said Mr Potts. "That's his weak point. He's very vain. All Italians are, that's why he wears that wig."

"Wig?" he typed. "Do you mean that that bounder's typically woggish head of hair is a toupee?"

"No doubt about it," said Mr Potts, pleased to be able to reveal Signor Baroli's best kept secret. "I'm very good on hair," he added, "and that's definitely false."

"Then by heavens we've got him, Henry," he typed.

"Have we?" said Mr Potts. "Good." Then to make sure he was thinking on the right lines, he added, "How?".

"We let Mrs Harris see him without it," said the suddenly evil voice of the late P. W. Arnold.

"But he always wears it," said Mr Potts.

"Then you must snitch it," he typed.

"I must what it?" said Mr Potts.

"Pinch it, Steal it, remove it, Henry."

"*Me*?" said Mr Potts aghast.

"Yes, you," he typed. "And then you must bury it in the garden."

Mr Potts suddenly regretted his moment of bravado when he'd said "just say the word."

"Oh dear," said Mr Potts. He lit a cigarette with an unsteady hand.

"Oh dear," he repeated. "I don't think I could. I mean . . . well, that's stealing," he added loudly.

His fingers flew back to the keys. "If you don't", he typed, "then I shall not only not help you to escape marriage to Mrs Baldwin, I shall do all I can to see you get to the church on time . . ."

Mr Potts inhaled deeply, and wondered what was wrong with his nerves. Would Dangerfield after all his adventures shirk from stealing an ageing Italian opera singer's toupee. Definitely not. Whereas he, Henry Wordsworth Potts alias the gallant Dangerfield, was going weak at the knees. What sort of man was he? Well, there was only one way to find out.

Stubbing out his cigarette, he gazed sternly at his reflection.

"I'm ready," he said.

"Good," he typed. "That's the spirit. Good man, Henry, now get down to his room."

Mr Potts nodded, then a worried frown crossed his face. "What if he's awake P. W. You know — reading or something?"

"Hang on," he typed, "I'll go have a dekko."

Mr Potts sat tensely waiting for the invisible shade to return then his fingers tingled and he typed.

"Just asleep and the damn fellow's wearing it in bed.

"Must be paranoid about his bald head," said Mr Potts, "but if he's actually wearing it how can I get it?"

"Good pull," he typed. "Like you do with sticking plaster. Probably won't feel it go and by the time he wakes up you'll be down in the garden and make sure you dig deep, Henry."

"Right," said Mr Potts, and before his nerve deserted him he headed for the door. Then a thought struck him. What if the glue wouldn't budge? Perhaps he could loosen it with just a drop of spirit. Picking up the whisky bottle, he crept out into the passage and walking on the side of the stairs to avoid making them creak, he headed for Signor Baroli's sleeping head.

Mr Potts paused outside Signor Baroli's door, a deep Basso Profundo snore greeted his ears and his heart suddenly started thumping so loudly that he was afraid it might wake the whole house. Unscrewing the top of the bottle, he took a gulp of the fiery contents and shuddered. No doubt about it, he was becoming an alcoholic. Not surprising really, after all, here he was in a boarding house in Streatham, engaged to the ugliest woman in the world, in between talking to a dead author in his room, rushing out to assist Sherlock Holmes and Bulldog Drummond and now about to steal a toupee from a sleeping opera singer. And that was just this week!

Mr Potts took another drink. Yes, if he wasn't an alcoholic he jolly well ought to be, the strain of it all was beginning to tell. Cautiously he opened the door and immediately his sensitive ear drums vibrated to the symphony of the sonorous snores that emanated from the bed near the window. Mr

Potts strained his eyes. Yes old P. W. was right, the toupee was lying on the pillow attached firmly to Signor Baroli's head.

Mr Potts crept to the side of the bed. Amazing, he thought, that anyone who snored so loudly could sleep through it. Mr Potts took another quick swig from the bottle, then cautiously reached out a hand and gently pulled at the black mop of hair. The snoring continued unabated and Mr Potts pulled harder, but apart from giving Signor Baroli a slightly Chinese look as the skin round his eyes strained upwards, there was little effect.

Well glued on, thought Mr Potts. The old campaigner P. W. had been right. A swift pull was the only answer. But first a little spirit round the edges. Mr Potts put a finger over the end of the bottle and shook it up. Then slowly and carefully he dabbed it round Signor Baroli's hairline. While he gave it a moment to work Mr Potts decided on his plan of action. A swift pull, then out of the door and down the stairs, through the back door and into the garden. Hide in the potting shed with the wig to make sure there was no pursuant. But pursued by a bald Baroli was unlikely, in case en route he met Mrs Harris, who would immediately reject him as a suitor because of his bald head. Yes a good plan, and worthy of Dangerfield at his best. Then a quick dig in the flowerbeds and a swift return to his room. Then prepare for a funeral after Signor Baroli had starved to death behind his locked door!

Mr Potts peered at the whisky-sodden hairline. Surely the fixative must have melted by now? Mr Potts placed the whisky bottle on the bedside table. He could almost feel P. W. Arnold standing by him, urging him on, as he grasped Signor Baroli's luxuriant locks with both hands. Here goes, thought Mr Potts, and pulled with all his strength. But instead of the sound of sticking plaster being removed, Mr Potts found to his horror that all he had succeeded in doing was to pull Signor Baroli up into a sitting position, and at the same time the snoring was replaced by a giant bellow that made the windows rattle.

Mr Potts' heart stopped beating and feeling as though he

was in the grip of some terrible nightmare, he ran from the room and down the stairs. Such was his confusion that he found that he had missed his room altogether, and he realised that his brain hadn't cancelled the instructions to his legs, which were faithfully trying to carry out the original plan of running into the garden with the wig. But it hadn't been a wig.

He was on the landing below his, and his heart still wasn't beating. How long could he live without any blood going to his brain? Mr Potts clenched his fist and struck his chest a couple of forceful blows. The sound of a door opening upstairs, followed by a bellow of rage, temporarily blotted out the worrying knowledge that he was dying and he opened the nearest door and stood behind it. To his relief he heard his heart pounding once more in his ears. Damn! He had left the whiskey bottle. They would find out that he, mild mannered Henry Potts, had turned into the prowling hair puller.

"I knew you'd come," said the emotion-filled voice of Mrs Baldwin. "But be quite darling, we mustn't wake Sydney."

Mr Potts' heart stopped again and he gave it an energetic blow with his fist, and as it started again a moment of inspiration came to him and, turning, he held out his arms and stared unseeingly ahead. With his unseeing eyes he noticed that Mrs Baldwin was wearing a pink silk nightdress and curlers and patches of cream on her face from which her bulging eyes stared back at him uncertainly. Next to her, on a camp bed, the inert, striped pyjama-clad form of Sydney lay sprawled, untidily, clutching a battered Teddy Bear.

"Henry?" whispered Mrs Baldwin anxiously.

Mr Potts continued to stare straight ahead and took a couple of paces forward then stopped.

"Oh," gasped Mrs Baldwin, her hand flying to her mouth. "He's sleep walking."

Mr Potts just managed to restrain himself from nodding. His ears had detected considerable activity on the stairway and he was about to need a good alibi and one that would excuse his unusual behaviour. As Mrs Baldwin got out of bed, Mr Potts tried not to blink as he noted a large bunion plaster on her left foot. He held his breath as she approached him.

"You are asleep," said Mrs Baldwin commandingly. "This is just a dream."

"A dream," murmured Mr Potts dutifully.

"And you must go back to bed," said Mrs Baldwin.

Mr Potts nodded gratefully and turned towards the door.

"But, before you go," said Mrs Baldwin, slipping round in front of him and speaking in an hypnotic whisper up his nose, "remember that you love Beatrice Baldwin with all your heart."

Cunning old bag, thought Mr Potts. It was Svengali and Trilby all over again.

"You are going to make her very happy," continued Mrs Baldwin, giving Sydney's sleeping form an anxious glance.

Mr Potts found it was becoming increasingly difficult to keep us his unseeing stare.

"I must go to bed now," he said in a low monotone.

A loud knock on the door made him blink, but fortunately it had also diverted Mrs Baldwin's hypnotic gaze. She opened the door to reveal to Mr Potts' unseeing eyes the irate face of the tousled haired Signor Baroli, the stern face of Mrs Harris and the pale anxious face of the lilac dressing-gowned Mr Leopold.

"Oh, he's here," said Mr Leopold.

"Shush!" said Mrs Baldwin, holding up her hand. "Mr Potts is fast asleep. He is," she said, lowering her voice, "sleep walking and it would be very dangerous to wake him in his present state."

"Oh yes," said Mr Leopold, "he could drop down dead."

"Sleep walking!" boomed Signor Baroli. "He is drunk. He has been in my room trying to pull my head off."

"Shush," said Mrs Harris, and peering closely at Mr Potts' unblinking eyes, she said, "Aye, he is definitely in a somnambulistic state. The late Mr Harris often got that way after a couple of drinks and Mr Potts was trying to get rid of his toothache with my best whisky."

"Then why does he put it on my head?" said Signor Baroli. "Smell my head, Mr Leopold." And lowering his head Signor Baroli thrust it under Mr Leopold's anxiously twitching nose.

"All I can smell is that horrible hair oil," said Mr Leopold.

"'Ave you come to play with me, Daddy?" said the voice of Sydney from just below Mr Potts' right elbow. The small Teddy was waved in front of his face.

Definitely time to wake up, thought Mr Potts, and with a wild cry that made Mr Leopold reel back against the wall he blinked his eyes and shouted.

"Where am I?" Then he slowly buckled at the knees, managing to delay his descent until his surprised audience caught him.

As willing arms helped him to his room, he explained he had dreamt that he was in the garden and had been trying to pull up a big weed.

"Thatta was my hair," said Signor Baroli, pointing to his head.

"No," said Mr Potts, feigning great surprise. "I'm terribly sorry, I can't think what came over me."

"And you poured some of ma best whiskey on Signor Baroli's head," said Mrs Harris reprovingly. "That must have been when I was watering the roses," said Mr Potts.

Once back in his room Mr Potts went straight to his typewriter and sat down. "My mistake, P. W.," he said. "It wasn't a wig." He fell asleep waiting for the reply.

Seven

The next morning, to Mr Potts' surprise, there was no sign of an armoured car waiting outside 69 Ranleigh Road with his pools win. Neither was there a registered envelope on the mat or a telegram of congratulations from the head of the pools firm. Perhaps his coupon had never arrived! In a state of great agitation, he telephoned Vernons in Liverpool and after a nerve wracking delay and after quoting his reference number to at least three girls he was assured that "'e was a winner" and that a cheque was in the post. Carefully entering the call in the large red telephone book by his bed, he skipped down the stairs to the kitchen from which his keen Dangerfield nostrils detected the delicious aroma of frying bacon and eggs.

Only the aged Elsie was in the kitchen and she gave Mr Potts a reproving look as he entered.

"Morning, Elsie," said Mr Potts.

"What was you up to last night then?" said Elsie. "Poor Signor Baroli is in bed wiv a bad 'ead, and Mrs H 'as got a 'angover. Wot on earf was you doing in 'is room?"

"I was in a somnambulistic state," said Mr Potts. "Er, that's sleepwalking and I was dreaming I was weeding the garden and pulled his hair."

Glancing towards the door, Elsie lowered her voice, "Pity you didn't put some weed killer on 'im," she whispered. "I never did like Italians, and 'e ain't arf got Mrs 'Arris in a state. She's been at the sherry bottle, an' that's always a sign." Elsie nodded as she placed Mr Potts' breakfast in front of him. "Give 'erself a hangover she 'as and still in 'er dressing room."

"I don't like him either," said Mr Potts, pleased to find an ally. Then lowering his voice, he continued. "And the sooner he goes the better."

"You know," said Elsie as she poured out Mr Potts' tea from a large battered silver pot bearing the impressive stamp of the Great Western Railway, "Mrs 'Arris is so worried about things she's got on to a friend who's a psychic, you know, one of them mediums."

"What for?" said Mr Potts breaking the rind off a stiff piece of bacon.

"To find out," said Elsie glancing up at the ceiling, "if the late Mr 'Arris approves. She's got an appointment 'ere on Friday. Comin' wiv 'er crystal ball and cards and all that."

"No," said Mr Potts through a mouthful of overdone egg.

"Yes," said Elsie. "course, I don't believe in all that mumbo jumbo stuff, but ever since Mrs 'Arris did a musical version of *Blithe Spirit* at Bridlington she's been a firm believer in occultism."

"But," said Mr Potts glancing behind him to make sure they were alone. "But what if this woman says that it's, that . . ." Mr Potts gestured upwards with his fork, ". . . the late Mr Harris says it's all right?"

"She'll marry 'im," said Elsie. "You mark my words, Mr Potts, she'll marry 'im. She can't be alone forever, can she?" And as Elsie sat down next to him on one of the big wooden kitchen chairs Mr Potts thought how frail and tired Mrs Harris's faithful ex-dresser, confidente and maid of all work looked.

He reached out a hand and squeezed her thin freckled wrist.

"Not if we can help it though," he said.

"No sir," said Elsie and suddenly burst into tears.

"Now, now," said Mr Potts, lifting the corner of the checked tablecloth and dabbing her eyes with it.

"'Eel make 'er get rid of me," sobbed Elsie. "Although I only work for my keep, I don't get no pay you see, but I'm like family you see . . ." Elsie tried to continue but only managed an inaudible whisper. Mr Potts took off his glasses, raised the other corner of the tablecloth to dab something in his eye. Then, putting a comforting arm around Elsie's frail bobbing shoulders, he said in a low firm voice, "I promise you Elsie, she won't marry Signor Baroli if I can help it."

"Oh sir," said Elsie looking up with red-rimmed faded blue eyes and her frail hand held his with the trust of a small child. He swallowed hard and tried to imagine he was Dangerfield dealing with the problem.

"Now, what's this woman's name?" he said. "This friend of Mrs Harris's."

"Oh, it's not a friend of hers, sir, it's a friend of Signor Baroli's. 'E says she's the best in the country. In fact, it was 'e wot suggested it. 'E said if she was worried about wot the late Mr 'Arris would think this lady would put 'er mind at rest one way or the other."

"I see," said Mr Potts, and although he didn't tell Elsie he saw much more clearly than any clairvoyant the double game that the evil Signor Baroli was playing. He narrowed his eyes and took a sip of hot tea. Then he narrowed them even more as the nerve in his troublesome tooth reacted violently.

"Are you all right sir?" said Elsie.

"Yes, fine," said Mr Potts smiling bravely. "Excuse me, I'm just going to look up the dentist's telephone number." Walking stiffly upstairs to his room he shut the door and putting his head under the bedclothes, to avoid upsetting the hungover Mrs Harris, gave a mumbled howl of agony.

A short while later Mrs Harris had descended the stairs wearing a large pair of pink-framed sunglasses and sniffing a lavender scented hanky and had found Mr Potts crouching by the phone in the hall holding his face with one hand and with the other walking his fingers through the Yellow Pages.

"Good morning, Mr Potts," said Mrs Harris. Then hopefully, in a faint voice she added, "I hope you are looking for someone to repair the garden shed."

Mr Potts explained from the corner of his mouth that he was giving top priority to the rear molar that was causing great anguish. Immediately Mrs Harris insisted on phoning what she described as her personal dentist, A Mr DuCann in the High Street, and in her best Clydeside accent had insisted that Mr DuCann must see Mr Potts, the author, immediately. On the National Health, of course. And to be prepared for an extraction and to be sure to use the gas as Mr

Potts, the author, was a very sensitive person and if he lost a lot of blood to be sure to make him lie down before catching the bus home.

During the conversation Mr Potts' toothache had disappeared as suddenly as it had arrived, so it was with great trepidation that he now pressed the doorbell under the polished brass plate announcing that behind the Victorian facade lurked Mr Theodor DuCann, F.R.D.S., R.C.S., then in smaller letters — By Appointment to the Zoological Gardens.

However, the sight of the rosy cheeked nurse in the white starched apron cheered up Mr Potts and her welcoming, sympathetic smile could not have been warmer had he been a travel-weary monk arriving at a remote mountain nunnery.

"Hello sur," she said with a strong West Country accent, "are you the one that's urgent, from 69 Ranleigh Road?"

"Yes, that's me," mumbled Mr Potts through the gloved fingers he held over his mouth the keep out the cold and followed her into the antisceptic aroma of the hall.

"The author," she said excitedly as she helped him off with his long brown overcoat.

"Er, yes," murmured Mr Potts.

"Well my name's Glenda, an' it's my first day 'ere. I just started. I'm from Kingsteignton in Devon. I come up yesterday on the train." She announced the news as though the very distance she had travelled and her means of locomotion would fire an author's imagination.

"Well done," said Mr Potts.

"That's where the cider apples come from," she said as she stood on tiptoe to hang his coat up on the hallstand.

"They do indeed," said Mr Potts, noting that her blue shirted bosom appeared to be trying to escape round the sides of her starched apron.

As he entered the empty waiting room with a brave smile he hoped that the spirit of the late P. W. Arnold was with him. Then perhaps in the next adventure her magnificent cookers would spring out into Dangerfield's strong brown hands. Then he frowned. With his luck at the moment, she'd probably turn out to be his daughter and he'd get 10 years hard labour! Picking up a frayed *Paris Match* to practise his French, Mr Potts sat down and read with interest that the Russians had entered Berlin and that the war was nearly over. He'd just got down to reading a rather good love story in *Woman's Weekly* when the door opened and Glenda appeared and spoke in a whisper.

"'Ees ready sur, now," she announced.

As he got up Mr Potts noticed the roses had disappeared from her cheeks and her small hands were shaking.

Poor girl he thought, new to the job and worried about me. "I'm going to be all right, Glenda," he said comfortingly, and taking off his glasses rose athletically to his feet and with typical Dangerfield drawl, he added, "I'm not afraid of a little pain."

"Oh, it's not you, sur," she replied holding open the door. "It was the last gentleman. It were all the blood. I wasn't expecting it."

Mr Potts clung to the doorway for support as his knees gave way. "This way sur," she said heading across the hall. Mr Potts took a deep breath and reminded himself again that to think Dangerfield was to be Dangerfield.

The cigarette smoking, bald headed, green plastic coated Mr DuCann who was drying his hands on a none too clean towel, was slightly taken aback by the speed with which his next patient entered and even more startled when the thin grim looking figure, with distraught hair, threw itself into the chair and lay back and rapped out in a deep staccato voice, "My name is Potts. I have a tooth that needs examining. Do whatever is necessary." With that the figure threw back its head and gripped the arm rests with great force, opened its mouth and closed its eyes.

Mr Potts felt as though his stomach had shrunk to the size of a hard boiled egg, but he was determined to show no fear. For this is how Dangerfield would behave, except of course Dangerfield had perfect teeth. He heard the rustle of plastic as Mr DuCann approached, then the chair shuddered and went up with a series of jerks and stopped. Mr Potts heard the sound of metal clinking, followed by the sound of rushing water. He screwed up his face and pressed his eyelids even more tightly together. As long as he couldn't see anything he'd be all right.

A curved metal nozzle was forced between his teeth, that had somehow become clenched and his saliva began its noisy disappearance up the suction pipe.

"Open wider," said the deep voice of Mr DuCann.

Mr Potts opened his mouth so wide he imagined he must look like a snarling trophy on the wall of Dangerfield's gun room.

"Now," said the voice, "I'm going to use this thin metal probe. Tell me when I find the right tooth."

As Mr DuCann started his survey Mr Potts found the strain of keeping his eyes closed too much, and opening them he found himself staring up a very hairy pair of nostrils, under which a top lip twitched with concentration, revealing a set of nicotine-stained false teeth that seemed to be attached to a set of extra large, pale plastic gums. Probably keeps his better set for private patients thought Mr Potts.

Then a pain, so acute, that he couldn't cry out shot through his jaw. His legs thrashed violently and struck something solid and Mr DuCann's hairy nostrils disappeared from view and under them his pursed lips whistled noisily.

"That was my shin," said the stern voice of Mr DuCann.

"Sorry," gasped Mr Potts.

"Pain killer," said Mr DuCann.

"Yes sur," said Glenda, and as she sorted through the various array of hypodermic syringes Mr DuCann pulled up his striped trouser leg and anxiously examined a red mark just above his suspender.

Mr Potts sat gripping the arms of the chair with hands of steel, and stared in horror at the large needle protruding from the syringe in Mr DuCann's hand.

"This," said Mr DuCann, "will not hurt you."

Seeing Glenda's reassuring smile Mr Potts steeled his nerves and gave what he intended to be a low attractive chuckle of derision at the suggestion that he minded a little pain, but all that came out of his throat was an unattractive rattle that caused Glenda and Mr DuCann to exchange an anxious glance.

Clearing his throat he waved hopefully towards the gas cylinders in the corner. "I thought that perhaps gas . . . " he whispered.

"Not on a long job like this," said Mr DuCann, his hand hovering over Mr Potts' mouth. "The tooth might break when I get the forceps on it and if you swallow it and it lodges on a lung . . . " Mr DuCann's voice suddenly disappeared into the distance as Mr Potts fainted into merciful oblivion.

When he came round he was lying on the sofa in the waiting room. Still hazy, he wondered if this was one of Dangerfield's many adventures. No doubt he had just rescued this rosy cheeked maiden who peered down anxiously at him.

"Don't worry, my darling," he whispered, wondering why his lips seemed so large and unwieldy. "You're safe now." He tried to raise an arm to stroke her cheek comfortingly, but the effort was too much. He tried to recall the adventure that had laid him so low.

"It were the biggest one I've seen," said the grateful heroine.

"Was it?" said Mr Potts frowning with concentration. Surely he hadn't comforted her already and couldn't remember. Then in a flash it all came back.

"My tooth," he said.

"Yes," said Glenda.

"So he's come round," said the voice of Mr DuCann from the doorway. Mr Potts weakly turned his head. In the doorway his adversary held a silver dish and advanced with it.

With Glenda's help Mr Potts struggled to his feet; he felt stronger every second. Fancy fainting like that, in front of a beautiful young girl. He adjusted his thick unwieldy lips into what he hoped was a brave Dangerfield smile.

"I hope," he said, "that the self-induced trance I put myself into made your task easier."

"Oh yes," said Mr DuCann with a sardonic smile. "It came out first pull." As he spoke he produced from behind his back a small silver dish. Mr Potts just had time to note that it appeared to contain a blood-stained fossil of enormous size before another self-induced trance caused him to fall into a bottomless cavity.

The tale of Mr Henry Wordsworth Potts' bravery in going to the dentist was the main topic of conversation at the dinner table at Ranleigh Road and Mr Potts, after a light lunch of hot milk taken through a straw, followed by an aspirin and a deep sleep until teatime, now felt well enough to recount in detail how the roots of his tooth, which reached almost to his left eye, had given Mr DuCann one of the toughest battles of his dental career. At the end of the tale Mr Leopold was holding his jaw and wincing in sympathy. "You're so brave," said Mrs Baldwin.

Mr Potts waved his fork and gave a lopsided deprecating smile before inserting a sliver of well-cooked sardine into the right hand corner of his mouth. Then throwing his head back, like a feeding sealion, he swallowed it without chewing.

"Oh do be careful there isn't a bone in that," said Mr Leopold.

"Yes, be careful daddy," said Sydney. "And could I have the tooth to put under my pillow?"

"Whatta for?" inquired Signor Baroli, dramatically raising his bushy eyebrows.

"It's for the little tooth fairy," said Mr Leopold. "They take your tooth and leave sixpence, all while you're asleep."

"I expect you still do it, eh, Mr Leopold?" boomed Signor Baroli, giving Mr Leopold a hearty nudge and then he threw back his head and let out a crockery rattling laugh.

"If you don't believe me," said Mr Leopold coldly, "why don't you pop yours under the pillow tonight and give it a try?"

The smile disappeared from Signor Baroli's saturnine countenance. "You think these are false?" he said and baring his large teeth for all to see he gripped them between thumb and forefinger and tugged fiercely at them.

"Mine," he announced. "All mine."

"Well they're so good," said Mr Leopold with mock admiration, "you could hardly tell them from the false ones."

"How are you feeling now, Mr Potts?" said Mrs Harris, hurriedly changing the conversation.

"Fine," said Mr Potts trying to hide the enjoyment he'd

had from the Leopold-Baroli exchanges.

"I have some good news," said Mrs Baldwin.

"And what is that?" said Mrs Harris.

"I've managed," said Mrs Baldwin, "to get tickets for all of us to go to Pollock Bros. Christmas dance."

"No," said Mr Leopold.

"Yes," said Mrs Baldwin, "and it's on Saturday."

"I must go to the hairdressers," said Mrs Harris.

"I'll book you into the Salon," said Mr Leopold, "and do you personally." Then squinting at her through half closed eyes he added, "I think a Madame Pompadour style."

"I didn't mention it before," said Mrs Baldwin, "in case I could only get one for Henry. But there were some cancellations in corsetry and I've managed to get us all in. Oh, and by the way, it's black tie of course."

"Magnificent," boomed Signor Baroli, "I shall get mine out of the mothballs."

"Fancy keeping a black tie in mothballs," said Mr Leopold.

"My dinner suit," said Signor Baroli, "in which I have performed before the crowned heads of Europe . . ."

"Not to mention being held over for an extra week at the Pier Ballroom at Margate," added Mrs Harris.

"I'm afraid," said Mr Potts, "I shan't be able to go. You see I don't possess an evening dress outfit."

"Me neither," said Mr Leopold. "I think they're rather de trop today. But I could wear a bow tie with my dark herringbone suit."

"I'm sure that would look very nice," said Mrs Harris.

"I can't go," said Mr Potts.

"But Henry," said Mrs Baldwin. "I've told everyone in my department about you."

"I don't have a dark suit," lied Mr Potts hoping Mrs Harris wouldn't remember his blue one with the patched elbows.

"Stand up," said Mrs Harris. Mr Potts rose guiltily. She had remembered the suit and was going to expose him.

"Yes," said Mrs Harris gazing at him with a critical eye. "Yes, I think one of the late Mr Harris's tail suits would fit you. We may just have to take in the waist, lengthen the trousers and the sleeves a wee bit."

"I'll help," said Mrs Baldwin. "I'm very good with a needle and cotton."

And so, after dinner, Mr Potts found himself in Mrs Harris's private lounge dressed in the late Mr Harris's best tail suit. While Mrs Baldwin gathered the trousers at the back and inserted a large safety pin Mrs Harris inspected the cuffs, announcing that there was plenty to let down and that all Mr Potts' worries were over.

"But nobody wears tail suits any more," protested Mr Potts.

"More fool them," said Mrs Harris. "They look most elegant."

"Maybe we could cut the tails off," said Mrs Baldwin.

"I wouldn't hear of it," said Mrs Harris. "It cost nearly £10 from Ellis Bros. in the Strand in 1930 and that was a lot in those days. And anyway," she added as Mr Potts opened his mouth to back up Mrs Baldwin's suggestion, "who knows, the style might come back!"

Leaving Mrs Harris and Mrs Baldwin hard at work on the late Mr Harris's tails, Mr Potts joined Mr Leopold and Sydney in the lounge watching a commercial for washing up liquid.

"I thought you'd gone to bed," he said sternly to Sydney.

"Oh please. Can I stay up to watch the film, Daddy?" said Sydney with what Mr Potts decided was a particularly irritating whine.

"No," said Mr Potts. "Off to bed."

"No," said Sydney. "I won't".

Mr Potts narrowed his eyes. "I don't think your Mummy will be pleased to hear you've disobeyed me." Holding open the door and pointing towards the stairs he repeated, "Bed, Sydney. Now!" To Mr Potts' concern, Sydney burst into tears and buried his small face in the faded cushions of the leatherette settee.

"Oh dear," said Mr Leopold, tearing his eyes away with difficulty from the Bronze Blonde Giant in the loincloth that was advocating Jamaica Rum. "Oh dear," he repeated, "he's crying."

Mr Potts hurriedly closed the door in case Mrs Baldwin heard how cruel he was being.

"Well, only for a little while, Sydney," he said. "Just this once." Sydney's tears vanished as though by magic and running up to Mr Potts he threw his arms round his waist.

"Thank you, daddy," he said. "I love you."

Mr Potts gazed helplessly at Mr Leopold, who nodded approvingly.

With a deep sigh Mr Henry Wordsworth Potts sat down and with Sydney on his knee watched Fred Astaire singing in top hat, white tie and tails, as he danced athletically with Ginger Rogers. He wondered how well Fred would have done if he hadn't copied Dangerfield's style of dancing and how much better old Fred's suit looked than the late Mr Harris's ancient tails, that were at this moment undergoing major alterations for the Pollock Bros. Christmas dance.

During the Prime Minister's party political broadcast Mrs Baldwin entered and removed a thumb-sucking, semi-conscious Sydney from Mr Potts' pins and needles-ridden knee.

"Your dinner suit's going to look ever so smart," said Mrs Baldwin.

"Oh good," said Mr Potts trying to sound enthusiastic.

"We have a crisis on our hands," said the Prime Minister gazing sternly into the Harris T.V. Lounge. "And we must tighten our belts."

"I've taken your seat in," said Mrs Baldwin, "and Mrs Harris is letting down the sleeves."

"We must," said the Prime Minister, gazing directly at Mr Leopold, "use our natural resources."

"I'm making my own bow tie," said Mr Leopold. "I've found a whole length of black silk I didn't know I had."

"I have every reason to believe," said the Prime Minister, "that we will pull through and I believe the young people must be allowed to have their say in our efforts to build a better, brighter Britain."

"Goodnight," said Sydney.

"Goodnight," said the Prime Minister.

"I don't like the Prime Minister's hair," observed Mr

Leopold as Mrs Baldwin ushered Sydney out of the door. "It doesn't suit him, it's too long."

The doorbell ringing interrupted any possible discussion as to whether or not it had been wise for the Prime Minister to appear with long hair.

"Now who's that?" said Mr Leopold, turning the volume down and going to the door. He peered into the hall. The bell rang again.

"Coming," shouted Elsie.

"A small woman in a big hat," murmured Mr Leopold over his shoulder. Mr Potts heard Signor Baroli's voice booming in the hall.

"Ah," vibrated the voice, "Madame Le Strange, how wonderful you could come."

"How do you do, Madame Strange?" quavered Elsie's voice. "May I take your fur?"

"Ta dear," said a hoarse Cockney voice.

"It's a spiritualist," said Mr Potts. "She's a friend of Baroli's."

"Oh my word," squeaked Mr Leopold in an hoarse whisper. "How exciting."

Over the shoulder of Mr Leopold's Fair Isle sweater Mr Potts saw a small woman in a wide brimmed hat, covered with artificial flowers from which a dead bird peered morosely; she wore a long, moth-eaten fur coat and an ancient dog of indeterminate parentage sat patiently watching her as she fought strenuously to extricate herself from the sleeve, helped by Elsie and Signor Baroli.

Mrs Harris opened the door of her Private Lounge.

"Ah, there you are," said Mrs Harris, and seeing Madame Le Strange's predicament, she waved Elsie aside and with a swift pull freed Madame Le Strange's arm, umbrella and most of the lining of the ancient fur coat. The dead bird bobbed in gratitude.

"Ta," said Madame Le Strange, and picking up her green canvas holdall, she pointed to the open door with her umbrella. "In 'ere?" she inquired.

"I think," said Mrs Harris using her best Clydeside accent, "Thaat you will find the atmosphere in my Private Lounge most conducive due to the many momentoes of the past." Then seeing the dog, she paused. "But, perhaps . . ."

"I'll leave Wellington out here," said Madame Le Strange. "'E's very psychic and tends to 'owl when he senses a vibration."

"Oh really," said Mrs Harris opening the door. She gestured Madame Le Strange to enter, then she paused and whispered to Signor Baroli.

"Aren't we going to be invited?" mumbled Mr Leopold anxiously.

"I'll ask them," boomed Signor Baroli and Mr Leopold hurriedly shut the door and pulling out a pink comb ran it through his golden locks. "We're in," he said.

Mr Potts just had time to fling himself into the chair and fix an interested gaze on a ladies' deodorant commercial, when Signor Baroli entered. Mr Potts and Mr Leopold dutifully allowed themselves to be attracted by the loud hiss from the doorway. "Amici," boomed Signor Baroli in a sepulchral whisper, "would you care to meet on of my dearest friends and perhaps one of the greatest living spiritualists, who has paid us a visit?"

"I certainly would," said Mr Leopold.

"Why not," said Mr Potts, and as they followed the large figure across the hall, he wondered just how well Signor Baroli's old friend had been briefed to say her crystal ball revealed that a Basso Profundo was about to come into Mrs Harris's life forever.

As they entered, Elsie was busy pouring out the sherry. Mr Potts noticed she looked very pale and the decanter in her hand was rather unsteady.

"Madame Le Strange," said Mrs Harris, "may I present Mr Leopold, who has been a regular here for some time; and Mr Henry Potts, the author, who had a tooth out only this afternoon."

"'Ello dears," said Madame Le Strange, lighting a bent cigarette which she had produced from her holdall.

As Mr Potts took in Madame Le Strange's sharp ferret-like features, straggly ginger hair and heavily rouged cheeks, he wondered how he could foil the plot that was unfolding before his eyes.

"Make yourselves comfy round the table," said Madame Le Strange, "and we'll see if we can contact our departed loved ones what are no longer 'ere."

"We'd better get Mrs Baldwin," said Mrs Harris.

"'As she bin departed long?" inquired Madame Le Strange, seating herself at the piano.

"She's upstairs putting her son to bed," said Mr Potts.

"Oh, said Madame Le Strange from behind a cloud of smoke. "Well let's get in the mood while we're waiting. Everyone know ''Ark the 'Erald Angels Singin'?"

"A magnificent number," boomed Signor Baroli.

"It's their favourite," said Madame Le Strange pointing at the ceiling. "And they always come when I render it." With her cigarette clamped firmly between her lustreless teeth and the bird bobbing in two-four time, Madame Le Strange threw back her head and burst into song in a shrill off-key voice. This was immediately drowned by the deep vibrant tones of Signor Baroli, who sang with one hand on the piano and the other on his hip.

Mrs Baldwin, her eyes bulging more than usual, entered during the moving encore suggested by Signor Baroli. As the last notes died away Mr Potts felt sure there could hardly be a departed spirit who had not heard the rallying call to come down for a chat.

"Magnifico," panted Signor Baroli, mopping his brow with a crumpled red hanky.

"This," said Mrs Harris, "is Mrs Baldwin, who was upstairs."

Mrs Baldwin smiled uncertainly.

"Mrs Baldwin, this is the famous Madame Le Strange."

"Clairvoyant, medium and cards read," added Madame Le Strange rising from the piano. "Anyone got an ashtray?" she inquired.

Mrs Harris turned to Elsie. "Get Yorrick," she said.

"Yes Madam," said Elsie, opening the doors of a tall cabinet as she searched through a number of newspaper-wrapped pieces of china.

"What's happening?" whispered Mrs Baldwin.

"Seance," said Mr Leopold. "Exciting isn't it? I'm only sorry that I don't know anyone who's dead."

"No one is dead," said Madame Le Strange, "only departed. Now please be seated and all 'old 'ands."

Mr Potts found he was holding on to Signor Baroli's hand which felt uncomfortably hot and Mrs Baldwin's which felt uncomfortably friendly.

Elsie, who had almost disappeared into the cabinet, gave a gasp of triumph and produced an off-white pottery skull and removing the top section, to which a lighter was affixed, she placed it on the table.

"Oh, I like that," said Madame Le Strange. "Very rococo."

"The late Mr Harris won it at tombola," sighed Mrs Harris. "He used to put his cigar through the eye socket," she exclaimed, "while he rehearsed on the pianoforte."

"As it was so personal," said Madame Le Strange, "It'll help with the vibrations." And sitting down she stubbed her cigarette out in the skull. Mrs Harris replaced the top and as the dying smoke drifted out of the nose and eye sockets, Madame Le Strange, held out her hands with a jingle of lucky charms and completed the circle.

"My guide is a ten-year-old Red Indian boy," she explained and, throwing back her hat, she inquired in a hoarse voice if Bald Eagle was there or not.

"A bit young to be bald," observed Mr Leopold.

A number of shushes greeted his remark. "Come in Bald Eagle," said Madame Le Strange. "You are with friends."

Mr Potts strained his keen Dangerfield ears for a reply, but apart from Signor Baroli's heavy breathing, the ticking of the grandfather clock, and Mr Leopold's stomach rumbling, he heard nothing.

"Pardon," said Mr Leopold.

"Yes he's here," said Madame Le Strange, "'e's 'overing."

Mrs Baldwin looked up nervously.

"Say 'ello to him," commanded Madame Le Strange, "to let 'im know we're friends."

"Hello Bald Eagle," said Mrs Harris.

"Welcome," murmured Signor Baroli.

"'Ullo," said a hoarse voice from Madame Le Strange's

throat. "It is I, little Bald Eagle, speakin' to you"

"'E's here," confirmed Madame Le Strange in her own voice.

"Deep voice," said Mr Leopold. "How old is he?"

"Shush," said Mrs Harris, "and say hello."

"Hello there," said Mr Leopold addressing the ceiling.

Mr Potts who had been keeping a close eye on Madame Le Strange's teeth to see if they moved, nodded to Mrs Baldwin.

"Hello Bald Eagle," she said. "I've got a little papoose," she added.

"Yer, I know," croaked the hoarse voice.

Trying to keep a straight face, Mr Potts murmured his welcome with downcast eyes.

"'Ave you," said Madame Le Strange, "a message for us?" She cocked her hat to one side and listened to an inaudible reply. "Oh what luck," she said.

"I didn't hear him that time," said Mr Leopold.

"It was personal for me," said Madame Le Strange. "And 'e's conveyed that the late Mr 'Arris is 'ere and wishes to communicate."

Mrs Harris gave a start and Mr Potts narrowed his eyes. Should he voice his suspicions? That this woman was a fake. But the excited look in Mrs Harris's eyes that gazed expectantly towards the flypaper affixed to the chandelier convinced him that he had left it too late.

"'E's standing by," said Madame Le Strange, then glancing at Mr Harris's photograph on the piano, she continued, "Big man, large 'tash and 'e's in 'is tails."

"He died in his favourite concert suit," said Mrs Harris in a whisper. Mr Potts repressed a shudder at the news.

"'E's very 'appy," said Madame Le Strange. "'E's smilin' and givin' a thumbs up."

"I can sense him near me," said Mrs Harris.

"I was his best friend," said Signor Baroli.

"You still are," said Madame Le Strange. "'E's pattin' you on the shoulder."

"I can feel," said Signor Baroli.

Mr Potts felt Mrs Baldwin's hand tighten on his and glancing at her he observed that her eyes had developed an almost supernatural bulge.

"I can see something," she whispered. "Something misty."

"She's psychic, she can see 'im," said Madame Le Strange approvingly.

"I think it's just the cigarette smoke," said Mr Potts, blowing hard and dispersing the grey cloud that hung over the table. Madame Le Strange gave him a piercing look. "Now, where was we?"

"My friend, Mr Harris, likes me," reminded Signor Baroli.

"Oh yes, and 'e would like you to make Mrs 'Arris 'appy," murmured Madame Le Strange.

This is it, thought Mr Potts, and as he contemplated uttering a strangled cry, followed by his collapsing on the floor to break up the meeting, a remarkable thing happened. The table suddenly rocked like a raft on a rough sea and then, to the accompanying gasps of surprise the loudest being from Madame Le Strange, it rose in the air and hovered.

"My Gawd!" croaked Madame Le Strange. "What the 'ell's goin' on?" Then with a crash the table returned to terra firma accompanied by a shriek of dismay from Mr Leopold.

"My foot!" he complained. Then his expression froze as he looked at Madame Le Strange. Some invisible force seemed to possess her and her head fell back as she went rigid in her chair.

"She's gone," whispered Elsie. Signor Baroli stared anxiously at the inert figure.

"She's gone into a trance," said Mr Leopold.

Madame Le Strange's jaw gave a convulsive twitch and then a voice spoke, a voice that sent tingles down Mr Potts' spine.

"Beware of Signor Baroli," it said.

"Good heavens," said Mrs Harris. "I'd recognise that voice anywhere."

Elsie gave a gasp. "It's himself," she said.

"Who is thees?" said Signor Baroli anxiously.

"My name," said the Voice, "is Mr P. W. Arnold, and you, sir, are a bounder, a liar and intent on luring Fiona into matrimony in order to get your hands on the deeds to 69 Ranleigh Road."

"Oh," gasped Mrs Harris, "surely not."

"Outrageous," spluttered Signor Baroli. Then shaking Madame Le Strange, "Wake up you old fool," he shouted.

"And," continued the relentless voice, "I advise Mrs Baldwin that she will be much happier if she . . ."

But to Mr Potts' dismay before the words which he was sure were going to put Mrs Baldwin off him for life could be completed, Madame Le Strange succombed to Signor Baroli's rigorous shaking and opened her eyes.

"Blimey," she said, "What 'appened?"

"You gave us a message from the dead," said Mr Leopold. Then crossly to Signor Baroli, "Why did you have to spoil it? It was just getting good, they were just saying that Mrs Baldwin would be much happier about something . . ."

"When I married Mr Potts," said Mrs Baldwin, "that's what they were going to say."

"Rubbish," said Signor Baroli. "all rubbish."

"'Ow dare you!" said Madame Le Strange, her dead bird bobbing angrily.

"I recognised the voice distinctly," said Mrs Harris, staring at Signor Baroli.

"So did I," said Elsie. "'E died 'ere, upstairs. Ever such a nice gentleman. Very fond of you, Mum, 'e was."

"I 'ave to be goin'," said Madame Le Strange. "There is an hatmosphere 'ere I don't like."

"What a shame," said Mr Leopold.

Mr Potts viewed the departure of Madame Le Strange and the aged Wellington with mixed emotions. On the one hand it was clear she had, with the assistance of P. W. Arnold, saved Mrs Harris from Signor Baroli, but on the other hand she had, it would seem due to her untimely awakening, inadvertently cemented his tie with Mrs Baldwin.

Eight

The meeting broke up in some disorder, Signor Baroli telling Madame Le Strange to go back to the pier and assuring Mrs Harris that he had suddenly realised this woman was a charlatan and, now he came to think of it, a part-time ventriloquist. After Madame Le Strange's departure, delayed in the hall by her loud insistence for the five quid Signor Baroli had promised her, Mrs Harris closed the door of the Private Lounge and refused to open it to Signor Baroli's continuous knocking.

Brushing aside Mrs Baldwin's invitation to a drink to discuss the encouragement they had received from the other side, Mr Potts entered his room and headed for the typewriter. He had a few words to say to P. W. Arnold. Almost before he sat down, his hands flew to the keys.

"Sorry Henry," they typed, "the old fool woke up just as I was about to tell Mrs Baldwin what a mistake she was making."

"I wish you'd told her first," said Mr Potts.

"Never mind," he typed, "I've had an idea to save you, and," confirmed the gleeful voice of the late author in time with the keys, "I don't think Mrs Harris will listen to that bounder Baroli any more."

"That's all very well," snapped Mr Potts, "but what about my predicament?"

"You have £600 on the way," reminded the keys, "and another exciting adventure and if you conduct yourself with the bravery and skill that you have so recently demonstrated I'll have you out of the woods in no time."

Mr Potts swelled visibly in front of the washstand. The words bravery and skill leapt from the typewritten foolscap like neon signs.

"Your progress has been closely observed," he typed, "by a dear friend of mine, the late Mr H. G. Wells, whose visionary prowess demonstrated in his stories has been more than vindicated since his arrival here, and who has very kindly come up after a lot of thought I might add, with a splendid answer to your problem."

Mr Potts gave a low whistle of surprise. Fancy that, H. G. Wells had been concentrating his massive intellect and visionary powers on to the problem of how to get rid of Mrs Baldwin, a problem which no doubt made writing *The War of the Worlds* seem a piece of cake.

"He's one of my favourite authors," said Mr Potts enthusiastically.

"And mine" typed the keys.

"I particularly enjoyed his books on war games with toy soldiers."

"I don't think I read those," said Mr Potts apologetically, "but I'll get them." Mr Potts made a hurried not on his pad. If old H. G. was going to help him the least he could do was to read all his works.

He suddenly found he'd dropped his pencil and his hands had flown back to the keys.

"The work that will concern you," he typed, "will be The Time Machine and you will be instructed in its operation when the time comes."

So that's how he was going to escape from Mrs Baldwin. The Time Machine must really exist and he, Mr Potts, would be told where to find it. He'd jump in, pull the starter and the centuries would roll back and he'd hide in the Dawn of History, battling with dinosaurs, dressed in a fur rug, all to escape marriage to Beatrice Baldwin of Pollock Bros., a high price to pay but well worth it.

"As a matter of fact," he typed, the late author's voice whispering approvingly in his ear, "you're not too far off the mark." Mr Potts frowned. "I was exaggerating of course," he said. "er, how exactly . . ."

"Cross the bridge when we come to it," tapped the keys. "First you have an adversary who for centuries has struck terror into the hearts of those brave enough to venture into his lair. A creature of cunning, a monster in human form, an indescribably evil thing, whose lust for blood is insatiable — warm, human blood."

Mr Potts gave an involuntary shiver and tried to remove his fingers from the keys, but they continued relentlessly, relaying the unwelcome details.

"A Phantom of the Night, created by the gentleman now standing by my side, the late Mr Bram Stoker who has kindly consented to allow me to pit Dangerfield against . . ."

Mr Potts muttered the name, "Dracula?".

"But who else?" he typed. "And at this very moment in the year 1929 based on a suggestion by the late Mr Damon Runyan — bracket, story by me, end of bracket — in his mist-shrouded Carpathian Castle, is awaiting the arrival of beautiful Miss Lovelips Van Dorn, former hatcheck girl and do-gooder from the Half Moon Club, New York City, and now, since checking his fedora, constant companion of Jo Bullits Braigan, Chicago's leading anti-prohibitionist, whose disagreement with his Sicilian connections as to the cost of the liquor they were loading onto his ship, SS Panama, caused him to flee in his former partner's custom built Cadillac convertible, spraying his pursuers with a handy equaliser in the shape of a trusty Thompson from the back seat, while Miss Lovelips wrestled bravely with the wheel, wishing a five dollar tip had not made such a deep impression on her good nature. But what was Miss Lovelips Van Dorn doing arriving at Count Dracula's castle?"

"What indeed," murmured Mr Potts as he adjusted his mind to the already complex situation.

"By chance," rapped the keys and the late author's voice confirmed the coincidence, "on a narrow twisting Carpathian mountain road, the incredibly handsome features of Captain Gregory Dangerfield, partly masked by the white sharkskin driving helmet and a pair of Daswunderbarnatch Goggles by Optik of Obergurgle, glowed tensely in the reflected green light from the dashboard of the giant two-seater Isotta Fraschini (coachwork by Castagne) which Dangerfield was testing for the works, and as he negotiated, with wrists of steel, the twisting, tortuous mountain pass, the vast outside exhausts thundering like tearing calico in his ears as his slim, brown hand selected the gears with unerring precision, while his keen eyes flick fearlessly like blue lightening piercing the rushing shadows. Little does he realise that once again somewhere on the chessboard of fate destiny had taken a hand in his affairs and that that destiny was about to meet him head on round the next corner."

As the sound of the keys died away Mr Potts found himself desperately searching for the footbrake of an ancient motor car, which was careering down hill at an alarming speed. The words, too fast to jump out and fancy testing a car in this weather, leapt through his mind. Then, through a hole in the mist, his electric blue eyes perceived a corner and gritting his teeth and wondering just how effective the test he was about to put his sharkskin helmet through would prove, he turned the wheel and closed his eyes. But even through the lids he could see the glow of the oncoming headlights, yet the impact seemed to take a number of years. Mr Potts opened his eyes just in time to see a black convertible driven by a girl with fair hair and staring eyes. Next to her a man with a big hat, also with staring eyes and then the crash mercifully coincided with oblivion.

Mr Potts came to with a splitting headache. Suddenly he remembered two pairs of eyes staring over the headlights, then nothing. He put a hand to his head, it felt rough and his hair was missing. Had he gone through the windscreen and scalped himself? Then with a sigh of relief he realised he still had his sharkskin helmet on and appeared to be lying on a cold hard surface. He raised his head and opening his eyes slowly noted with regret that he could only see out of one of them, and that eye observed that he was on the floor of some sort of vault, and that the shadows dancing on the walls were caused by a flickering candle, on an oblong table, or was it a table? No. The shape seemed familiar. His eye concentrated on it for a moment longer before his brain decoded the message. It was a coffin.

Mr Potts closed his eyes and considered Dangerfield's plight. He was obviously in some sort of church. Perhaps because his heart in the shock of the crash had been beating so slowly he'd been given up for dead. Not an uncommon case in primitive countries where medical knowledge was scanty, and here he was missing his left eye. No longer would it flicker about like blue lightning. Instead it had probably fallen over a cliff or under a bush. Of course, the late P. W. Arnold would write a chapter where Dangerfield had a glass one fitted that would stare relentlessly at adversaries as his good one looked for a way out from a seemingly impossible situation.

The late P. W. Arnold's voice broke into Mr Potts' melancholy reverie. "Dangerfield's magnificent physique had survived the crash," said the Voice, "his mental faculties were as alert as ever. Taking off his helmet and goggles, he examined his surroundings more closely."

Mr Potts removed his goggles and stared with relief at the oil-covered left eyepiece of Optik. Mr Potts staggered to his feet and headed for the small arched door. There was no handle and it did not bulge as he applied Dangerfield's strong shoulders to it. Bending down he peered through the keyhole. No key. So he'd been locked in to wherever he was; but where was he? Mr Potts glanced at the coffin again and with echoing footsteps walked over to it. During the short journey he glanced down and became aware that he was very smartly dressed in a long leather driving coat. "By Hoggs of Holborn," intoned the late author's voice, "and the driving boots are, of course, as always by Mirello of Milan."

Mr Potts gazed down at the coffin and as he did so the hair under the turned up collar of his driving coat became as stiff as a shaving brush for, quite clearly in Gothic letters, he saw a name had been carved. He blinked and ran his hand over it to make sure he wasn't imagining it. But unmistakeably the letters spelt 'Dangerfield'. His coffin. He'd been right after all. He'd been presumed dead, left in a mortuary and his coffin had already been inscribed. He must let the authorities know at once that he had once again cheated the headless horsemen. Taking the candle, Mr Potts ran to the door, kicking it forcefully with his boot, shouted for help. But apart from hurting his toe, the result was negligible.

"Taking," said the echoing voice of his creator, "the lock pick from the false heel of his left boot, and making sure his trusty silver duelling pistol by William Binns & Son of Nuneaton was still strapped to his right leg, Captain Gregory Dangerfield, with the expertise and speed of an ex-Sing-Sing peterman working on a locked bedroom door behind which he suspects Rudolph Valentino and his wife are not playing gin rummy, soon heard the familiar click as the lock snapped open."

Mr Potts, panting slightly from the tussle with the ancient lock, put the pick in his pocket and pushed the door open. He stepped into a narrow arched corridor.

"I'm alive," he shouted, but apart from a flurry of wings and an ear-piercing squawk like chalk across a blackboard all was silent as a grave. Mr Potts paused for a moment to consider the situation.

It was quite obvious what had happened. After his head-on collision he had been left for dead and Miss Lovelips and her companion, Bullits whatsit, had somehow found their way to Count Dracula's castle and were no doubt in great personal danger. Meanwhile Dangerfield's inert form had been discovered by a passing peasant, presumed passed on, and had been laid to rest in the crypt of a local church to await the arrival of the local monks for a murmured Matins.

Mr Potts congratulated himself on his powers of deduction, worthy of Holmes after a long session on the violin. In fact, he hardly needed P. W. Arnold's brief commentaries to outline the plot. It was all so simple. Now all he had to do was to raise the alarm, gather some villagers and storm the castle and rescue Dracula's prisoner and no doubt receive his just reward from Miss Lovelips, who from her nickname promised to make up for the recent dearth of sexy heroines, with bursting bosoms and a backlog of unrequited passions.

As for Bullits whatshisname, he would deal with him in Dangerfield's inimitably cool perfunctory style. A crisp left to the jaw followed by a contemptuous grin in a downwards direction. Yes, all was clear and time now to unleash the world's most perfect fighting machine. Jutting his jaw as heroes do, an effect contrived by clamping his bottom teeth outside his top ones, and peering sternly through his spectacles, Mr Potts, with the candle held high above his head, marched along the seemingly endless corridor. Must be a church, he thought, or perhaps it was a monastery. Yes, of course, didn't they have long underground passages leading to nearby nunneries where the nightly naughties took place? No wonder they all went bald so early!

Suddenly he came to a door at the end of the passage. Taking a deep breath, he gripped the wrought iron handle. Dare he open it? Would dozens of sex-crazed nuns, all looking like Sophia Loren, leap on to his body, pinioning his arms, while others disappeared under his big driving coat, chanting *Ave Maria* to drown his cries for help to the Mother Superior. He paused considering the picture carefully. Yes, put like that it was worth a try.

Mr Potts pulled the door open, and stared in amazement at the magnificence of the chapel he had so sacreligiously filled in his mind with sex-crazed nuns. Hidden lighting shone down on a magnificent open black coffin with gold handles, raised on a dais and covered with red silk. Behind it dark red velvet curtains rose up to be lost in the gloom of the invisible ceiling. Mr Potts unlocked his teeth and gave a low whistle of surprise and admiration.

Making a mental note that affiliated members of the Vatican had no expense spared when it came to saying goodbye, then curiosity getting the better of him, he tiptoed towards the dais and putting foot on the marble step, Mr Potts peered into the coffin and nearly dropped the candle. For, dressed in black and looking very pallid, was none other than Mr DuCann F.R.D.S., R.C.S. whose spirit, judging by his appearance, was now in the great cavity in the sky.

But of course, in the plot which for the moment was more real than Ranleigh Road this was clearly the body of Jo Bullits Whatsit, mercifully killed in the crash and because of his powerful Italian connections given a much more expensive funeral than Dangerfield, whose exploits had clearly been omitted from the local press. In fact, come to think of it, they hadn't even put him in his coffin. Just left him on the floor. Strange. But all was clear again.

The only apparent survivor was Miss Lovelips Van Dorn herself, who had somehow staggered to Dracula's castle for succour and to put it bluntly had been sucked or was about to be if the daring Dangerfield, in the shape of Henry Wordsworth Potts, did not get there in time. But of course he would. Because he always did. All he had to do was to find the castle. Just as he was about to turn away, the pale eyelids of the late Mr DuCann popped open revealing two liquid black eyes that sparkled feverishly in their pale sockets.

Mr Potts' heart missed a beat. Old Bullits was still alive. Strange how the local peasants assume that anyone lying down in a wrecked car must be dead.

"Take it easy Bullits," said Mr Potts, remembering the sort of James Cagney dialogue that this sort of person would feel at home with. Then he added the words "Old pal" to show that for the moment they were bound by the common bond of an imminent rescue operation.

Stiffly, Mr DuCann started to sit up and Mr Potts put a helping arm round his shoulders.

"Take it easy, bud," he murmured, "you may have concussion."

The feverish unwinking eyes stared intently at him and Mr Potts felt the first twinge of goose pimples behind the ears. One of Mr DuCann's white hands gripped his arm with remarkable firmness for one who looked so unwell and to Mr Potts' surprise Mr DuCann pursed his red lips and hissed at him a sort of endless letter "S". As he hissed his feverish eyes that never blinked stared into those of Mr Potts.

"S, something," said Mr Potts nodding encouragingly. "Save the girl?" he added helpfully.

The eyes stared unwinkingly at him and Mr Potts tried to think what else began with S.

"Stay with me, er I'm unwell?" He was quite unprepared for the other hand which reached out like a white talon and gripped him by the throat and the large red mouth with the giant eye teeth that sprang open in the white face just under his nose and made him drop the candle in the coffin. With a croak of alarm, the next moment he was pushed against the chest and shoulders of his adversary, whose eyes now gazed in the direction of his jugular with great interest.

Perhaps he wasn't Bullits after all. The teeth were unusual, to say the least, and he was not surprised to hear the voice of the late P. W. Arnold confirming his worst fears with the words, "And so, caught off guard, Captain Gregory Dangerfield struggled for his life in Count Dracula's tomb. But even his great strength could be of no avail against this monster whose superhuman powers were about to overcome the forces of light and whose teeth were about to sink in to the lean brown handsome neck that would soon lose its colour. Was its owner about to become Dangerfield the undead, doomed by destiny to roam the ramparts of Dracula's castle until a stake through the heart released him forever from this fate worse than death?"

The picture conjured up by the voice of the late author plus the news that he was fighting a one-sided battle caused the strength to drain from Mr Potts' arms.

If only he had a cross. If only he'd eaten a garlic sausage to sustain him on his drive, but now it was too late and to his horror he literally fell into his adversary's arms. His sudden collapse also seemed to take the Count by surprise and mistiming his bite he sank his teeth into the upturned collar of Mr Potts' driving coat by Messrs Hogg & Co. of Holborn, which to his relief successfully withstood a test not normally called for in everyday wear.

Pulling Mr Potts' collar aside with a snarl of annoyance, Mr DuCann opened his mouth again and paused, savouring for a moment his victim's helpless plight, and in that moment Mr Potts regretted ever borrowing the late author's typewriter, for without it he would no doubt be sitting in a comfy leatherette settee watching the weather forecast on telly and thinking about filling his hot water bottle and making a cup of cocoa. Instead he was about to lose his suntan the hard way and change his diet forever.

"But," said the distant voice of his creator, "Dangerfield's instinctive Zen savvy for self-preservation that had caused him to drop the lighted candle had paid off, for the Count's left trouser leg was on fire."

Mr DuCann opened his mouth even wider and his eyes took on an even more feverish look. Beating desperately at the flames with his cloak he omitted a piercing scream.

Suddenly released from the vicelike grip, Mr Potts leapt back and turning ran towards an archway at the far end of the room. Throwing a fearful glance over his shoulder, Mr Potts imprinted on his mind the picture of Count Dracula's chalk-white eyes as he stepped hurriedly out of his smoking trousers, revealing blood red suspenders supporting his black socks, and then he was through the arch and bounding up a flight of stone stairs that stretched in a corkscrew spiral endlessly above him.

As he ran, the late P. W. Arnold's voice urged him on. "In a wild bid," it said, "to save the girl, Dangerfield's powerful legs, that had outdistanced Mahbuli the 8-foot tall Zulu warrior and his tribe of troublemakers as Dangerfield carried the limp, voluptuous body of Angela Goaling the zoologist whose attempt to study at close quarters the mating habits of the orang utang had ended so surprisingly, now pounded like pistons as he took the stairs two at a time."

Mr Potts mentally added the information that these legs would be heading straight for the front door and if they were as good as he was led to believe they would continue nonstop to the coast.

The stairs seemed endless and Mr Potts found the spiral course was making him dizzy. If only he could come out of his trance at the typewriter and have a rest.

"Even Dangerfield's magnificent lungs were beginning to tire," said the Voice, "but just when the stairs seemed endless he saw a door." Mr Potts pulled himself wearily up the last few steps on all fours. His overworked heart pounded like a muffled anvil under his big coat and he could feel his blood literally pulsing through his jugular vein. The thought struck him that if he got bitten now, while his heart was so active, all his blood would leap out at once and he'd never even make being a vampire.

Reaching the door, he turned the ancient iron handle and pushed. The door didn't move. Glancing nervously down the gloomy well of the stairs he wondered if Dracula had already changed into a bat and was even now gaining altitude before readjusting his appearance at his side. He felt a feeling of deep resentment that old P. W., who was supposed to equip his hero for any eventuality, had omitted a collapsible butterfly net in the lining of his big coat. Quickly assembled, he could have trapped the Count in his bat guise and jumped on him with his special driving boots, saving himself and the world from this ghastly menace. He pulled again and the handle came off in his hand. As he stared at it in horror a series of high pitched squeaks came to his ears; the squeaks became louder and there was no doubt that Mr DuCann was using his built-in radar to guide him up the stairs.

"The reason Captain Dangerfield paused," said the Voice, "was that he was considering carefully the possibility of waiting for the Count to materialise and then, taking him by surprise, throw his steel-like arms round his adversary, hoping to catch him off balance and, locked together with the demon of darkness, plunge into the bottomless pit of eternal oblivion, with his inimitable chuckle of derision and a pang of pity in his gallant heart that he would never again see Nola the Nautch Dancer whose virtuosity on the saxaphone had given him so much pleasure. Would her rendition of "Tiger Rag" whilst swinging from the chandelier of Grand Hotel, 13A Sebastepol Street, Warsaw, be his last haunting memory?"

Mr Potts shook his head vigorously.

"Or," continued the Voice, "should he push open the door and for a moment retreat?" The word push jerked Mr Potts out of his trance. Why couldn't P. W. have mentioned which way the door opened earlier? Mr Potts threw his shoulder at the door and his feet scrabbled on the concrete as he pushed with all his strength while the squeaking got nearer. Finally with the protesting creak of ancient hinges, the door opened to reveal a large gloomy hallway with a fire in a grate, almost as big as Mrs Harris's garage, and a massive wooden table on which the body of a young girl with fair hair lay spread-eagled, secured by ropes. A long squeak in the close vicinity of Mr Potts' left ear made him clap a hand on his neck and slam the door behind him. To his horror there was no sign of a bolt or lock. How could he keep Dracula at bay? "Without a second's hesitation," said the voice in his ear, "Dangerfield rushed to the table and despite its enormous weight threw himself against it, closing his eyes, his muscles bulging."

Mr Potts gripped the seemingly immovable piece of furniture, noting with surprise as he did so that it was Mr DuCann's assistant Glenda who stared at him with hope in her blue eyes. Then gritting his teeth and hoping he wasn't going to slip something, he tried to move it.

"Using," said the Voice, "the secret method of releasing adrenalin taught to him by Mighty Molehill Magee, the amazing circus midget, whose feat of lifting a fully grown gorilla above his head was the main talking point at his funeral later that day, Dangerfield pushed the table towards the door."

To Mr Potts' surprise the table did move and then to his horror he saw the door start to open. He had a brief glimpse of the trouserless Mr DuCann, cape held out like wings as he prepared for a dramatic entrance, when the edge of the table caught the door and closed it, trapping the flapping edge of the cloak as it did so. Mr Potts collapsed for a moment, his head on the table, with a sigh of relief.

"Gee baby, thanks," exclaimed a grateful voice. "Am I glad to see you."

And looking up Mr Potts realised that Miss Lovelips Van Dorn, with her blouse disarranged and missing a vital button or two, was well worth risking a slipped disc for. Her neck looked attractively unpunctured so far. All he had to do was untie her and what was the expression . . .? Beat the hell out of the joint.

"Delighted to be of service," said Mr Potts in his best gritty Dangerfield drawl. "Allow me to deal with these tiresome bonds." "That jerk with the wild dental work sure gave me the creeps," confided Miss Van Dorn.

"That," said Mr Potts grimly, as he wrestled with a reef knot, "was Count Dracula."

"Are you sure?" said the wide-eyed Miss Van Dorn. "He didn't look like Bela Lugosi to me."

Mr Potts observed that the power of the silent screen had

already exerted its grip on the public. He started nervously as a frustrated howl came to his ears and he glanced up to see the piece of cloak caught in the door was being tugged by its irate owner. A rending sound indicated that Dracula's wardrobe was having a bad night.

"I don't think I've introduced myself," said Mr Potts enjoying his temporary immunity to danger and the grateful glances being cast towards his handsome face as he undid the last knot. "I am Cap . . . "

Miss Van Dorn's mouth, true to her nickname, was hot and moist. "She ended further conversation by kissing him passionately on his chisled lips," murmured the late author. Was there a note of envy in his voice? "And thrusting her magnificent bosom up under his chin, she felt the heady euphoria that all women experienced when they kissed Dangerfield for the first time, and not even her strict convent upbringing could prevent her from ripping off her clothes and giving herself away to the rhythm of the drums in her head."

"No, no, not now," said Mr Potts hurriedly. "Think of the convent," he added as he disentangled himself from her grasp and helping her off the table said, "We've got to get out of this place."

"I love you, baby," gasped Miss Van Dorn, staring at Mr Potts and reminding him of a rabbit that's seen a stoat. He must tone down Dangerfield's kisses, they were dynamite.

"Yes, of course," he murmured, then arched his head to one side, listening, and Miss Van Dorn followed suit.

The absence of any sound from beyond the closed door filled Mr Potts with deep forboding. Perhaps Mr DuCann had resumed his bat role and found another exit. He glanced towards the fireplace. Could he even at this moment be flying head first down the flue? A hissing sound in the close proximity of his neck turned his legs into elastic bands and with a cry of alarm he pulled up the collar of his driving coat.

"Hot milk and an aspirin," said a familiar voice.

Mr Potts suddenly felt quite dizzy as he tried to turn around. When he did so he found himself face to face with a worried looking Mr Leopold who held a brown enamel mug in one hand and two aspirins in the other.

"Should be in bed," said Mr Leopold, his mouth twitching with concern. "I knocked and knocked and I thought you said something. Are you cold?"

Mr Potts suddenly became aware that he was clutching tightly the turned up collar of his sport jacket.

"Er, oh yes, fine," he gasped, releasing it. "Er, just finishing a story. Got a bit engrossed with the plot."

"Working too hard," said Mr Leopold, shaking his head. "Now, take these and get some byebyes."

"Thanks," said Mr Potts and putting the aspirins on the end of his tongue, he took a gulp of hot milk.

"All of it," said Mr Leopold indicating the mug. "It's good for you."

As Mr Potts drank his milk under Mr Leopold's watchful eye, he wondered what he'd say if he knew of the desperate plight his fellow boarder was in — a plight which unless he, Mr Potts, in the guise of Dangerfield, was successful in escaping from this could be their last meeting. For if he failed, as P. W. had pointed out before, he would be found dead over the keys of the ancient Imperial. But wait! Even worse, he wouldn't be dead, he'd be a vampire. The full horror of his fate struck him. He'd be mild-mannered Henry Wordsworth Potts by day, then at night, drawn to the typewriter like a magnet, he'd type his fangs in and using a red carbon spend his time terrorising young maidens. No more torrid love affairs — for as soon as he put an arm around them and opened his mouth they'd be off with a shriek of alarm not unlike his last unsuccessful relationship with Miss Martin of the Electricity Board. Finishing the milk, he handed the mug back to Mr Leopold.

"Thanks," he said. "That was very good of you."

"No more work tonight," said Mr Leopold wagging an admonishing finger. "All work and no play makes Jack a dull boy," he added. Then reaching the door he whispered. "Like it shut?"

"Yes please," said Mr Potts.

"Night night," breathed Mr Leopold. "Oh, and by the way," he added, "they weren't aspirin, they were sleeping pills. Hope you're not cross but it's so hard to get you to take care of yourself." With that he disappeared and closed the door.

Sleeping pills? Mr Potts put a hand to his middle and gazed at his distraught reflection in the washstand mirror. Sabotaged just when it was getting exciting. Now he'd have to go to bed and wait until tomorrow for the final chapter in the epic struggle. The next minute his hands had leapt to the keys and his fingers were once again drumming with alacrity.

"I can't go on with the story now," gasped Mr Potts. "If I fall asleep in it . . . "

But before he could amplify his fears he found himself back in the Great Hall holding Miss Van Dorn by the wrist as she gazed trustingly into his troubled blue eyes. Mr Potts headed for two tall iron-studded entrance doors that barred the way to freedom. But before he had covered half the distance a thunderous knocking on the very same doors stopped him in his tracks. Either Mr Leopold had come back for his mug or Mr DuCann had found a way out, but appeared to have forgotten his front door key.

Above the knocking Mr Potts heard the voice of the late author, P. W. Arnold: "Dangerfield," it shouted, "took stock of the situation. Someone or something was at the entrance. To flee to the cellars would be fatal, but dare he risk the final denouement with Dracula in the presence of this frail creature?"

"Jeeze," said Miss Van Dorn. "Do something daring or it'll be curtains for both of us."

At the far end of the hall Mr Potts spotted a flight of stairs. Once up those there would be nowhere to go except out of a window. Perhaps down the ivy, if there was any ivy. But didn't plants show a marked reluctance to live in Dracula's presence? His attempt at constructive thought was interrupted by Miss Van Dorn's decision to scream hysterically. Almost simultaneously the pounding at the door ceased.

"Lovelips baby," cried an unfamiliar voice. "Hold on, I'm coming in."

The next moment the staccato sound of shots fired in quick succession filled the air and a great number of holes appeared round the handles of the doors. Then there was another loud thud and they swung open and with mixed emotion Mr Potts observed that standing in the doorway, wearing a black fedora, white scarf and ankle-length overcoat, beneath the hem of which a sturdy pair of correspondents peeped, and clutching purposefully his equaliser in the shape of a Thompson sub-machine gun, was none other than the late Mr Harris, whose portrait at this moment was gazing at the back of Mr Potts' head as he sat in a trance at the washstand at Ranleigh Road, typing his destiny.

"Heist 'em high," said Mr Harris, waggling the gun barrel at Mr Potts, "and over to the wall. I don't want to do Lovelips any harm when you get yours."

"You got it all wrong Bullits," exclaimed Miss Van Dorn. "This guy was getting me out of the joint. It is this Bela Lugosi's hideout," she added.

"What's that junk?" said Mr Harris.

"It's Count Dracula's castle," said Mr Potts in a crisp rather matter-of-fact voice. "Thought to be but a figure of imagination but all too real in the flesh."

"Give me the English on that," said Mr Harris wrinkling his brow.

"He still lives," said Mr Potts.

"Pull the other one, bud," said the late Mr Harris spitting unattractively on the floor, "it's got bells on."

"I've seen him," squeaked Miss Van Dorn, glancing nervously over her shoulder. "Let's get out of here, it's spooky."

"Good thinking," said Mr Potts introducing an urgent note into his voice.

"Relax baby," said Mr Harris, and pressing the butt of the Thompson against his hip he curled his finger round the trigger. "So long bud," he added.

"Was this, as they say, curtains for Dangerfield?" murmured the voice of the late author in Mr Potts' ear. "Alas, his big driving coat prevented him exercising his lightning draw, said to be faster than that of ace High Hickenberry, the poker playing preacher who, shot through the heart by a heavy loser, still managed to draw and cock both colts and play an ace from his cuff before cashing in his chips for keeps. But did this gangster realise just who he was?"

Of course, thought Mr Potts.

"Just a moment," he said, "I don't think you realise who I was, I mean, am."

"If you're a Fed," said Mr Harris, "you're going to get it in the knees first." And to Mr Potts' dismay he distinctly saw the trigger finger twitch.

"Er, hold it," he gasped. Then recovering slightly he attempted a toothy devil-may-care grin. "I am," he said deepening his voice for maximum effect, "Captain Gregory Dangerfield." He found to his dismay that he'd dropped his voice so much that it sounded like a run down gramophone record.

"Jeeze," said Miss Van Dorn. "That's right, I seen his mug in the papers."

"The guy," said Mr Harris wrinkling his brow, "who let the air out of Beauregard Brannigan, the much wanted kidnapper of Honey Hamilton, the Hogg Heiress from Houston?"

"The same," murmured Mr Potts casually.

"He was my brother," whispered Mr Harris.

"Goodbye, Lovelips," said Mr Potts closing his eyes, and praying earnestly that P. W. had equipped him with a bullet-proof waistcoat that he had forgotten to mention. He could then fall on the floor, or perhaps do a James Cagney run on his knees for the door before appearing to die in satisfactory agony with a supplicating hand on his adversary's two-tone footwear.

"If only he had had his bullet proof waistcoat," said the voice of his creator sadly. "But of course, Dangerfield hated to spoil the cut of his jacket by Henshaws."

The unkindest cut of all had to be a sartorical one, thought Mr Potts poetically.

"Now look here," he said "this . . .

He had meant to continue on the lines that this is only a story, I'm actually Henry Potts of 69 Ranleigh Road where you died over 20 years ago. Your girlfriend is the assistant to my dentist, who is of course Count Dracula who took my tooth out earlier today, that is today in 45 years' time — but before he could elaborate to clear the doubt that this story might raise, a familiar hissing sound came to his ears and Mr

Harris's open jaw and fixed stare passed him, confirmed that they were not alone.

"It's him!" shrieked Miss Van Dorn.

Mr Potts turned and saw Mr DuCann gliding down the last of the stairs raising his red-lined cloak in a menacing manner, at the same time baring his teeth as he continued to glide across the hall towards them.

Mr Potts' heart missed a beat. Why didn't Bullits fire? The same question also appeared to trouble Miss Van Dorn.

"Give it to him dummy," she yelled, and her familiar voice seemed to galvanise Mr Harris into action.

"Goodbye baby," said Mr Harris, and the next second a staccato burst of fire echoed round the vast hallway and empty cartridge cases cascaded over his correspondents.

Mr DuCann hissed even louder and continued without faltering as the fusillade continued.

"Impervious to lead, which cannot kill him," shouted the voice of the late P. W. Arnold, "Count Dracula sought revenge on those who had defiled his lair."

Mr Potts stared transfixed as the late Mr Harris in a final desperate effort hit Mr DuCann over the head with the barrel of his gun. The next second Mr DuCann's head bent down and pulling the white scarf aside he buried his face from view.

"This was Dangerfield's chance," said the familiar voice in his ear. "Time now to use his special bullet kept for just such an emergency."

Of course, thought Mr Potts, mentally blocking out the voice in case it spent precious moments describing other adventures in which he had used such a bullet. His hand searched feverishly for his pistol. Suffice it to know that only Dangerfield would keep a silver bullet in his gun, just in case. Finding it, he pointed the small twin barrels at Mr DuCann's back and pulled the first trigger. Mr DuCann paused in his efforts and turned and stared sternly at Mr Potts. Then, releasing his pallid victim, who sat down with a dull thud and leant glassy-eyed against the wall, he glided purposefully towards Mr Potts. With a great effort Mr Potts stood his ground and pointing in the general direction of Mr DuCann's heart fired the other barrel. Mr DuCann looked even more stern and reached out towards Mr Potts with his bloodless white hands.

"His special bullet," said the late, impatient voice of the author, "that he kept in the right heel of his driving shoe by Mirello of Milan."

Grinding his teeth with annoyance, Mr Potts turned tail and hopped hurriedly away as he tugged at the laces of his driving shoe. "Don't leave me," screamed Miss Van Dorn, and her footsteps echoed across the hall as he pursued the hopping figure of her saviour.

Pulling off his shoes, Mr Potts fumbled with the heel cautiously. Remembering how on the last occasion whilst hanging from the bell in the Notre Dame he'd cut his finger on the blade secreted there. With a click the bottom of the heel slid back to reveal the precious silver bullet. Taking it between thumb and forefinger, he turned and to his surprise found that Mr DuCann had stopped in his tracks and was staring malevolently at him. Was that a hint of fear in his eyes?

"Silver bullet," said Mr Potts. "I think you know what that means?" "I vos eggspectink zat," said Mr DuCann in what Mr Potts presumed was Transylvanian English.

"Zay all try zizz," and from a pocket under his cloak he produced a square object, no bigger than a match box on top of which appeared to be a tuning fork.

"Scientific progress hass its uses," said Mr DuCann, and pressing an unseen control he held the box so that the tuning fork pointed towards Mr Potts. An almost inaudible hum assailed Mr Potts' ears, then to his surprise the bullet twitched in his fingers, then left them, to reappear to the accompaniment of a ping on the prongs of the tuning fork.

"A magnet" said Mr DuCann, revealing a lot of fang to indicate his pleasure. "Vibrating on ze same molecular frequency as ze silver."

Mr Potts suddenly felt very tired. Could it be that the sleeping pill, given with the best intentions by Mr Leopold, could be the final nail in his earth-filled coffin? Mr DuCann glided slowly towards him like a bad dream.

"Fortunately," whispered the voice of the inventive author,

"in Dangerfield's other shoe, for just such a situation, was another bullet made of lignum vitae, the strongest wood in the world. It comes from South America and is even too heavy to float in water."

But before the late P. W. Arnold had started on his explanation regarding the peculiar properties of this vampire deterrent Mr Potts had begun hopping madly into the distance, followed by a puzzled Miss Van Dorn and a confident-looking Mr DuCann.

With a click the second shoe revealed its secret compartment occupied by a dark shiny bullet in its brass cartridge case. A wave of dizziness swept over Mr Potts as he peered through his spectacles trying to focus on the gun, which swam before his eye. Rapidly it appeared to have four barrels and in desperation he tried the middle two and was relieved to feel the bullet go home. Pulling back the hammer with his thumb, he turned. His head cleared in an instant as he found himself face to face with his adversary, who stood arms outstretched with an evil smile on his face. His liquid black eyes seemed to bore into Mr Potts' brain.

"Vi don't you shoot?" said Mr DuCann, as Mr Potts hesitated for even though he had been through many adventures as the gallant Captain Dangerfield, he couldn't recall ever staring into an adversary's eyes and killing him in cold blood. In the heat of battle, yes. But this was different.

"Dangerfield," said the urgent voice of his creator, "savoured his moment of triumph, and uttered the last words the Demon of Darkness would ever hear." The Voice paused and feeling that something rather memorable was called for, Mr Potts searched the dictionary of his mind. As he did so Mr DuCann's amazingly strong hands gripped him by the neck and his hot breath flamed Mr Potts' cheek.

"Goodbye baby," croaked Mr Potts and pulled the trigger.

The effect was dramatic. Mr DuCann let out such a blood-curdling scream that Mr Potts dropped his pistol. He found himself staring, transfixed, down Mr DuCann's throat. Then Mr DuCann seemed to shrink in front of his eyes. Still screaming, he staggered back towards the table and fell on it, his white legs dangling over the edge. Mr Potts blinked. Yes, no doubt about it, Mr DuCann was decomposing in front of him. The red suspenders suddenly slipped down Mr DuCann's withered legs and Mr Potts turned away from the nerve-wrecking spectacle and observed the inert body of Miss Van Dorn, for whom the proceedings had proved too much.

"Without a backward glance," said the late P. W. Arnold, "Dangerfield recovered his trusty duelling pistol and picking up the lovely Miss Lovelips Van Dorn ran for the door of Castle Dracula."

In a moment Mr Potts found himself pulling at the entrance door with Miss Van Dorn slung over his shoulder. As he did so a hissing sound made him glance round. The late Mr Harris was slowly pulling himself to his feet. His pallid face and feverish eyes were turned towards Mr Potts and the curious eye teeth he revealed, as he framed some words, confirmed that the cult of vampirism was not dead.

"Say, waddabout me?" exclaimed the late Mr Harris, obviously having trouble with his unaccustomed dentures.

But Mr Potts was already running on the most powerful legs in the world.

"To find safety and succour," murmured the delighted voice of Dangerfield's creator, "after killing the Count and leaving behind one of Chicago's leading anti-prohibitionists, doomed to roam the world of the night, suffering the greatest hell of all. For vampires only drink blood."

Nine

Mr Potts did not remember hearing another word, for semi-reality blended into a dream and only when awoke the next morning, with his head banging over the side of the wash-stand and one hand still on the keys, did he read, whilst he drank a hot cup of early morning tea, that he had made the village safely and had spent an amazing night at the Inn in the arms of a hatcheck girl from the Half Moon Club, whose amorous advances had apparently taxed even his great strength, for it appeared that he had fallen asleep just as she pulled the cord of his borrowed pyjamas.

One thing was clear. He must never again accept an aspirin from Mr Leopold!

At 8.30 the postman called. A moment later an excited Mrs Harris rushed up to Mr Potts' room and hardly bothering to knock, held out a long white envelope and in a broader Clyde-side accent than she normally used, she announced, "I think it's guid news thaat we have from the pools."

Mr Potts rose from his chair and stared at the envelope.

"The big win," added Mrs Harris nodding her head.

Mr Potts took the envelope gingerly and picking up a sharp pencil inserted it in the corner of the flap and slit it open.

"What a pity Mrs Baldwin and Mr Leopold have just left for work," said Mrs Harris.

"Yes indeed," said Mr Potts, pulling out the long crisp buff cheque, and holding it close to his nose gazed at the amount predicted by the late P. W. Arnold exact to the last penny. Mrs Harris looked over his shoulder mouthing the figure to reassure herself that her eyes had not deceived her. A moment later she hugged him and Mr Potts found himself doing an impromptu highland fling on the threadbare carpet watched by the feverish eyes of the late Bullets "Vampire" Brannigan.

"Six hundred and forty two pounds!" shouted Mr Potts. "Yippee!"

At the stroke of ten the doors of the National Westminster Bank opened to allow an impatient Mr Potts inside. Miss B Catchpole appeared temporarily speechless by the enormity of the sum as, under Mr Potts' watchful eye, she checked his paying-in slip.

"I'd like to have a word with the manager, when I have time," he murmured, "investments, that sort of thing. Oil seems strong at the moment."

"He'll be pleased you've paid your overdraft off," said Miss Catchpole. "He's been going on about that."

"He's not cashing another cheque, is he?" said a familiar voice. And the manager's face appeared behind Miss Catchpole. From its disapproving expression Mr Potts gathered that the manager regarded the question of his overdraft as a personal vendetta.

"'E's won the pools," said Miss Catchpole, £642.

The disapproving expression disappeared as though by magic and the face looked younger by some years.

"Good," said the manager. "We shan't be requiring an overdraft again."

Mr Potts found himself replying before he'd almost thought the words.

"You won't," he said, "because I'm transferring my account from this bank to Barclays Bank across the road."

The scratchy black pen he used to write out the cheque was the only sound to be heard in the ensuing silence his remark had created.

"When," said Mr Potts icily, blotting the ink, "when your superiors want to know why you have lost an old customer, tell them he was dissatisfied with the way you run this branch and has placed his capital elsewhere."

And so, with £619 in his pocket and feeling well over six feet tall, Mr Henry Wordsworth Potts, man of means, had unless his imagination deceived him the satisfaction of seeing the bank manager age rapidly again, before his eyes, as he left the counter for the last time and headed with echoing footsteps across the marble floor.

It wasn't until he was on the bus going home that he realised he'd forgotten to go to Barclays and that if any of the passengers knew what was in his pocket . . . He lowered his head, folded his arms and tried to look poor and anonymous at the same time — so successfully that the conductor even forgot to ask him for his fare.

On the kitchen table the money was counted out to the accompaniment of Elsie singing — "Pennies from Heaven" — and Mrs Harris saying how reckless of Mr Potts to carry so much money on his person and what about a month's rent in advance to relieve him of some of the responsibility?

The phone rang and Elsie answered it. It was Mr Leopold from the salon and amidst the excited chatter and sound of hair dryers Mr Potts gathered that Mrs Harris had telephoned Mr Leopold and Mr Leopold was telephoning back to say he was so excited that he was too overcome to do a decent blow wave and had nearly drowned a customer by holding her head under the tap while thinking what Mr Potts could do with all that money. Perhaps a honeymoon abroad? Mr Potts pretended not to hear the suggestion and shouted his goodbye.

As he put the phone down a sobering thought struck him. Now he had the money what excuse could he give Mrs Baldwin for not marrying her? What had happened to the late P. W. Arnold's offer of help? Where was it? And with a deep sigh he headed for his room.

Who could help him now? No doubt tonight at Pollock Bros. staff dance Mrs Baldwin would announce their betrothal officially and it would all be over bar the shouting. Then a quick "I do" in the Town Hall registrar's office and back to 69 Ranleigh Road for a honeymoon in his room. Or perhaps her room? Or would he, as Mr Leopold had suggested, have to use some of his winnings and take her away somewhere? Sitting down in front of the washstand he contemplated his anxious expression. Mrs Harris had already hinted that she had some pull at Mrs Featherstone's theatrical boarding house at Frinton-on-Sea. Would the old

MG get as far as Frinton? Suddenly he felt that he must escape now before it was too late. He could pack and leave now, with ready cash in his pocket, he could catch a steamer and go to Canada and start a new life — on the run. All he had to do was to leave a farewell note.

Ten

Inserting a fresh sheet of foolscap in the typewriter, he wound it round and poised his fingers over the keys. He'd just managed a capital "G" for goodbye when his hands were taken over by the familiar, invisible force and he found himself typing.

"Good heavens, Henry. What is the matter with you?"

"You promised to help," said Mr Potts reproachfully, "and now it's too late."

"Nonsense," he typed, and the late P. W. Arnold's optimistic tone confirmed his faith in the typewritten words. "Now," continued the Voice in time with the keys, "what would cause your bride-to-be to break off the engagement?"

"Heart attack?" suggested Mr Potts, hopefully.

"Her heart's as strong as an ox," he typed.

Mr Potts thought for a moment and shook his head.

"Nothing can save me." "What," he typed, "if she was swept off her feet by another man? Someone rich and handsome?"

"She doesn't know anyone rich and handsome," said Mr Potts.

"No indeed," he typed, "but someone rich and handsome knows her and who better to help you in your hour of need than the most handsome man in the world, Captain Gregory Dangerfield!"

"But how," said Mr Potts, running a hand through his distraught hair. "He only lives in the past, how can he . . . ?" "By using," tapped the keys, "an invention created by the gentleman standing by my side at this very moment. The late Mr H. G. Wells, creator of *The Time Machine.*"

Mr Potts stared at the typewritten words trying to

comprehend as his fingers continued.

"By using the Time Machine," they typed, "to transport Dangerfield to today. He can sweep Mrs Baldwin off her feet and you, quite rightly as the jilted lover, will have nothing more to do with her. It can't fail, Henry. For as we both know there is not a woman in the world who would not succumb to Dangerfield's charm."

"True," said Mr Potts, his heart beating wildly. "But how?"

"Now, this is the plan," whispered the voice and as the keys continued Mr Potts found himself watching P. W. Arnold's brainwave appear in print. No sooner was the picture of the scheme and his part in it firmly embedded in his mind than the room began to disappear and in an instant he was immaculately attired in top hat and tails, sitting in the driving seat of a magnificent Rolls Royce. Apart from the ticking of the clock on the dashboard, and the swish of the tyres on the open road, it was as silent as the room he had just left more than 50 years in the future.

"The immaculately attired and incredibly handsome Captain Dangerfield sat at the wheel of his 1920 Silver Ghost speed model," said the voice of the late author. The voice continued in an enthusiastic whisper, "Lightweight coachwork by Hibbard and Darrin with japanned leather roll back roof; the ultimate Barouche for long distance touring."

Mr Potts knew where he was heading and a signpost confirmed that Richmond was only five miles away. For it was at Richmond that the Time Machine was to be found, where it had lain since H. G. Wells' Time Traveller had created it and disappeared on it into the future. Now it was back again and waiting to transport Dangerfield into the future, to rescue Mr Henry Wordsworth Potts from a fate worse than death. As on other occasions, Mr Potts tried to get the whole thing into perspective. As he drove through the green countryside he saw this as being his most memorable adventure ever, for he was shortly to meet himself face to face.

Following the directions of the late P. W. Arnold, Mr Henry Wordsworth Potts, top hat tilted rakishly over his left eye and his chamois gloves lightly holding the steering wheel of the Rolls Silver Ghost, glided over Richmond Bridge. Mr

Potts had a quick glimpse of a rowing eight motionless and exhausted on their ragged line of sculls. Then old Father Thames swept them tiredly away for a bath and no doubt a great deal of beer.

He went on down Richmond High Street. Right turn and soon a left shortly followed by an instruction to halt. Mr Potts peered at the large old house behind the trees at the end of a gaunt cul-de-sac. He was rather surprised to find it still standing. But although the paintwork was faded and the tall hedges that hid the garden were in need of a trim, the well-oiled gates to the driveway opened silently to his touch and arriving at the large wooden garage he alighted again. Opening the doors with the key that was already in the padlock, he drove the shining Ghost in, stopped, then following P. W. Arnold's instructions Mr Potts donned a brown, knee-length, dust jacket, removed his gloves and hat and with the aid of the correct tool from the polished selection in the black wooden toolbox drained the water from the radiator. Then removing a number of wooden blocks from the boot, he jacked up the car and carefully inserting the blocks under the four corners, left it suspended.

Mr Potts hoped the precautions suggested by the late author would prove effective, as if things went according to plan, he'd be using it again in 45 years' time. Locking the garage and putting the key in his pocket, Mr Potts made his way across the overgrown flower beds towards the small outhouse at the back which housed the Time Travellers' laboratory.

Mr Potts found the door locked. Aided by the late afternoon sun, he peered through the dusty windows. He could discern a wooden bench and a vice and odd boxes with bits and pieces strewn about untidily on shelves, but nothing else.

"He'll be here, don't worry," said the comforting voice of the late P. W. Arnold.

"How does he know I'll be here?" said Mr Potts, "And where is he coming from?"

"He's coming from the past," said the Voice irritably, "or indeed, perhaps the future. It doesn't matter. The point is the late Mr H. G. Wells has kindly written an extra chapter to his story where the Time Traveller, who will as always remain nameless, helps the amazing Dangerfield to leap into the twentieth century to meet himself."

Mr Potts nodded and glanced round the overgrown garden. Who owned the house now? Perhaps the Time Traveller owned the freehold and could visit it in the future and use it as a base for operations. Yes, that's what he would do and if anyone asked who he was he'd just pass himself off as his own great grandson. He'd disappeared in 1872 and was no doubt popping up somewhere in every century.

Mr Potts' assessment of the Time Travellers' movements was interrupted by a loud report and a tile fell off the roof of the outhouse, narrowly missing his head. Leaping to the window and shading his eyes, Mr Potts observed a misty shape starting to take form near the bench, then a vibrating thing of glittering brass and ivory and astride it the shadowy figure of a grey-haired man wearing a Norfolk jacket and plus fours. The Man turned his face towards Mr Potts and though the late H. G. Wells had chosen to keep the identity of the inventor of the Time Machine a secret, Mr Potts had no difficulty in recognising the manager of the National Westminster Bank and his expression was no less anxious than when Mr Potts had withdrawn his account.

Jumping off the contraption the Time Traveller unlocked the door and breathed a sigh of relief.

"I'm glad you're here," he said. "It's so difficult to judge things to the moment and I hate being late. I was late for the Battle of Hastings — missed the whole thing by a week and I'd taken my camera. Most disappointing."

Mr Potts murmured his condolences.

"We must hurry," said the Time Traveller as he consulted the row of clocks on the Machine. "Such a lot for me to see and so little time. That is to say," he explained as Mr Potts climbed on to the Machine behind him, "so little time in my lifetime, which ended many years ago. Saw my own funeral, very moving affair. Of course, I wasn't dead, just presumed to be as I'd been missing so long. Funny thing about time travel is that one hardly ages at all, as long as one keeps travelling."

Mr Potts' bank manager sighed wearily.

"It's very tiring," he said frowning at the clocks and

adjusting a platinum rod.

It was clear to Mr Potts that being a Time Traveller wasn't exactly a laugh a minute.

"Hold on," said the Time Traveller.

Mr Potts glanced at the window and in that moment he saw a reflection of himself in his top hat and tails sitting on a weird looking contraption in a delapidated shed in Richmond, and wondered how he could seriously imagine, as he clasped his bank manager firmly round the waist, that he was a sane normal person. Well, if he was slightly mad he'd better stay that way to keep sane.

At the corner of the window, and under Mr Potts' fascinated gaze, a spider spun a web in a fraction of a second, then the room grew faint and hazy and in the twinkling of an eye it was night and then day and then faster still night again. Mr Potts clung on grimly; he felt as though he were on a giant switchback and he was aware that night was following day like the flapping of a black wing. To Mr Potts, as he held on for dear life, someone appeared to be playing tennis with the sun, so quickly did it move, until it became a streak of fire interspersed with the black bands of night. Until finally the swaying machine stopped and Mr Potts stared at the same dusty window. But now outside was dark. Was it his imagination or was the laboratory even dustier and some of the windows boarded up? The Time Traveller pointed to the array of clocks.

"It's Friday February 14, 1974," he said. "Nearly half past three in the afternoon."

"Dangerfield," said the welcome voice of the late P. W. Arnold, "thanked the Time Traveller and after synchronising their watches he bade them farewell and opening the door of the outhouse, he stepped into a veritable jungle of weeds and long grass."

The Time Traveller had obviously given up on the garden except for the small area around the door.

"Don't use this century very much," explained the Time Traveller, and he adjusted the setting of the centuries. "Spend a lot of time in the twenty-fifth century when earth has been invaded by an army of beautiful, sex hungry women looking for new males. They are from the planet Altar 17 in the Triad Galaxy and they've carried off most of the men, it's a despicable situation. I've nearly been caught myself, more than once."

Mr Potts was tempted, just for a moment, to suggest that he might accompany the Time Traveller to the twenty-fifth Century where he could not only escape the bug-eyed Mrs Baldwin from planet Earth but surrender his body to the beautiful invaders who appeared to be rearranging the destiny of the earth in such a satisfactory manner. But before he could even say goodbye, both the Time Traveller and the machine of Ivory and glimmering quartz started to vibrate and grow misty. A sudden gust of wind blew the door shut and, peering through the window, Mr Potts had a brief glimpse of the shadowy shape of the weird contraption and its rider before it disappeared altogether.

A few minutes later Mr Potts had inserted the key in the now rusty padlock on the garage door. With a protesting squeak it turned and a moment later he was busy with the jack and then with loving care he used a duster, to wipe the dust of nearly half a century off the immaculate coachwork. Apart from a few cracks in the leather it all looked as good as it had done a few minutes earlier in 1929. A sudden thought struck him. By now he must have flat battery.

"And so," said the comforting voice of the late P. W. Arnold, "with one swing of the starting handle Captain Dangerfield fired the engine, which thanks to magneto ignition did not need a battery."

Driving the magnificent Dangerfield Rolls in 1974 was an experience that Mr Potts would never forget, the admiring glances and the way other cars gave way to him.

"Like sail before steam," commented the late P. W. Arnold.

And here he was, the handsome Captain Dangerfield in 1974 heading towards the Hammersmith flyover in a 1920 Rolls that he'd brought from the past.

Forty minutes later Mr Potts swung the Rolls into Ranleigh Road. As he did so, he caught a glimpse of one of his bedroom windows on the side of the house. The light was on and he was no doubt hard at work typing this adventure. As he put on the handbrake he glanced at his reflection in the driving mirror and breathed a sigh of relief — he was still the desperately handsome debonair Dangerfield that had stared back at him from the mirrors. Stepping out of the car, with his heart beating like a trip-hammer, he opened the garden gate and headed for the front door and although he'd been through the plot with the late P. W. he found the thought of meeting himself, face to face, completely unnerving. And more to the point, was he — that is, Henry Wordsworth Potts the author — expecting him? Or rather, Dangerfield? He imagined himself at the washstand typing the words — and so, he rang the bell reaching out an immaculately gloved hand.

He rang it. Elsie answered the door and wiping her hands on her apron she gazed open mouthed at the figure on the doorstep. With a deft movement he produced his visiting card and handed it to her.

"Hardly able to believe her eyes," said the voice of the late author, "Elsie, the menial, bade the handsome stranger enter and called to her mistress."

"Gent ter see yer, Mrs H," screeched Elsie, then controlling her vowels and with exaggerated care, "Mrs Harris will be here heny moment."

Mr Potts caught a momentary glimpse of a small, bespectacled person with distraught hair and a pale anxious face peering at him over the bannisters from the first landing. It was a moment or two before he realised that this insignificant looking being was Henry Wordsworth Potts, the writer. He closed his eyes to lessen the shock. Then a familiar voice spoke.

"Guid heavens!" it said.

He opened his eyes to observe Mrs Harris with an outstanding corsage of plastic marigolds. Mrs Harris, in her full evening dress, glanced at the card.

"Guid heavens," she repeated. Then glancing up, "Captain Gregory Dangerfield, in person. I can hardly believe it."

"It's true," said Mr Potts, "I'm quite real."

"But," said Mrs Harris, "I thought that you, that is, he . . .

that is Captain Dangerfield was just a fictional hero of the late P. W. Arnold, who as you may probably know, spent his declining years in this very house and died in the room now occupied by Mr Potts the writer. Who, following in the late P. W.'s literary footsteps, is continuing to write about the very same character."

"My father, Captain Dangerfield," said Mr Potts, "was a close friend of the late P. W. Arnold and I determined that one day I would visit the house where my late father's late friend died."

"Come into my Private Lounge," said Mrs Harris.

"Thank you," said Mr Potts, pleased that the plot seemed to be going so well and hardly able to believe that Mrs Harris did not recognise him as Mr Potts, but only saw him as Dangerfield.

"And so," said the voice of the late P. W. Arnold, "we find Captain Gregory Dangerfield in the Private Lounge of Mrs Fiona Harris, who is praising the late P. W. Arnold, rogue elephant, world traveller, man of letters, homme fatal."

As Mrs Harris continued enthusiastically about the talents of her late boarder Mr Potts sat back in her best armchair, crossed his elegantly trousered legs and sipped her best Safeways Amontillado sherry and gazed round the familiar room with its familiar odour of mothballs and old furniture. The late Mr Harris peered admiringly at him from behind his Red Shadow disguise. Mrs Harris's eulogy was interrupted by a knock at the door. The knock was followed by a discreet, vibrating cough. Mrs Harris gave a tut of annoyance and it was clear to Mr Potts that Signor Baroli was still out of favour.

"Enter," said Mrs Harris.

Signor Baroli entered and close behind him came the rest of the Harris household.

"It was also clear," said the voice of the late P. W. Arnold, "that word had got out of a most unusual visitor to this small suburban dwelling.'

And in a trice Mr Potts found himself shaking hands with a beaming Signor Baroli, in full evening regalia (complete with Armistice Medal and Water Rat pin), an admiring Mr

Leopold wearing a smart dark blue herringbone suit and pink bow tie who shook Mr Potts with a rather clammy hand and stared very directly into his electric blue eyes, so much so that Mr Potts was relieved that his extremely handsome appearance in the house was only of a temporary nature. Then came Mrs Baldwin. She was wearing a gown of green and yellow with diaphonous lengths of grey chiffon round the neck and sleeves. The whole effect, aided by her bulging eyes, reminded Mr Potts of a fat, juicy insect breaking out of its chrysallis. He found the picture spine-chilling to say the least.

But not quite as spine chilling as the second appearance of the small bespectacled, weedy looking man in the overlarge dinner suit, whose pale face stared intently at him from the doorway. "And this," said Mrs Harris, "is Mr Potts, the author, who is writing about Captain Dangerfield."

Mrs Harris's voice died away in the background of his thoughts as he stared at himself in his role of Henry Potts the writer. Did he really look that insignificant? He was aware that Henry Potts the writer had extended his pale hand and taking it in his strong bronzed grip, he shook it consolingly. There was no doubt that in Henry Potts the author's eyes there were both recognition and admiration. But why wasn't he upstairs typing the plot? Or was he really Dangerfield living in the Twenties, who occasionally had a nightmare that he was this person Potts in the Seventies?

"And this is," said Mrs Harris. He became aware that Mrs Harris was still speaking to him. "And this is," repeated Mrs Harris, "Mrs Baldwin, who has just become engaged."

"Dangerfield," breathed the Voice in his ear, "took the lady's hand and kissed it." Mrs Baldwin nodded. Dangerfield Potts shook his head.

"Impossible," he murmured and raised an eyebrow quizzically to show how impossible it was.

"Why ees it impossible?" inquired Signor Baroli with a puzzled expression.

"Because," he whispered, "I, Captain Gregory Dangerfield, have — for the first time in my life — fallen deeply in love." And taking Mrs Baldwin's suddenly limp hand, he crushed it to the watered silk of his lapel.

"When," he murmured, in his most attractive Dangerfield drawl, "when one has looked into the eyes of a goddess one realises that destiny plays its hand in many strange ways."

He was suddenly aware that Henry Potts, the author, was staring at him open-mouthed.

"It does indeed, sir," said Mrs Baldwin breathing heavily.

"Gregory, please," he murmured encouragingly.

"She is virtually engaged," said Mrs Harris.

"Oh, what have I done?" said Mrs Baldwin gazing with distaste at Mr Potts the writer before returning her gaze to the face of the handsomest man in the world.

"Don't worry, Mrs Baldwin," he said.

"Beatrice," she murmured weakly.

"Don't worry, Beatrice. But before I go, Ivor Novello can express my feelings even better than I."

Sitting at the piano and selecting the sheet music from the top of the piano, Mr Potts in the role of the magic-fingered Captain Dangerfield accompanied his attractive, haunting voice in a heartfelt rendering of "Some Day I'll Find You". He noted with satisfaction that he was gazing at himself admiringly. Halfway through it, Mr Leopold fainted but no-one seemed to notice. Signor Baroli attempted to join in, but after a sharp kick on the shin from Mrs Harris, he vibrated into silence. As the husky tones died away, Mrs Baldwin tried to speak but emotion overcame her.

"Brilliant," boomed Signor Baroli.

"My late husband, 'the most famous Baritone', could not have rendered it better," said Mrs Harris.

"I'm sorry I missed most of that," said Mr Leopold grasping the leg of the piano and pulling himself sharply to his feet, "but it's rather warm in here."

A muffled sob came from the chaise longue, then Elsie blew her nose noisily.

"Better than Sir Noël," she announced.

"Dangerfield," said the Voice, "had, as always, his admiring audience in the palm of his hand, and finally acquiescing to their repeated requests he gave his renderings of "Tiger Rag,", "Happy Feet", "Home Town" and finally part two of the Brandenburg Concerto in C. Major.'

The applause ringing in his ears, Mr Potts the pianist flexed his aching fingers and stood up. He was pleased to note that Potts the author continued for some time after the rest.

"A night to remember," said Mrs Harris.

"I 'aven't 'eard better at the Halbert 'All," said Elsie.

"I shall buy a record of the Concerto tomorrow," said Mr Leopold, "Won't be as good, of course."

"Do you have an agent?" whispered Signor Baroli.

Another kick from Mrs Harris saved Mr Potts from having to answer. Instead, he picked up his gloves from the piano. "I must go now," he said, glancing at his watch, "er, I have an appointment."

"Oh, don't go," said Mrs Baldwin gazing up at him, and her expression reminded him of a starving bulldog that's just seen the juiciest bone in the world.

"I'm afraid it's goodbye," he murmured, "although I would prefer *au revoir.*" And after a brief search in the chiffon he found her hand and kissed it again.

"I'm on my way," he said, "to Australia."

"Australia," croaked Mrs Baldwin.

"Yes. To see how the Dangerfield gold, silver, copper and nickel mines are doing."

"My sister has a teashop in Wogga Wogga," announced Mrs Baldwin excitedly, and together with the rest of the Harris household she followed the dashing figure into the hall.

Turning, he addressed himself to Mr Potts. "Oh, by the way," he said, "could I perhaps see the room my father's friend, the late Mr P. W. Arnold, died in?"

"With pleasure Captain Dangerfield," said Mr Potts, "this way." And as he followed his thin wispy counterpart up the familiar stairs he felt a moment of deep regret that he couldn't be Dangerfield for always. But like the Time Travelling he had to keep travelling and his Time Machine was the ancient Imperial typewriter.

A moment later he saw it in its familiar place on top of the old marble washstand. His room looked incredibly small and spartan and the thin dressing gown on the back of the door contrasted sharply with his big warm monogrammed one back at Dangerfield Manor. Mr Potts, chronicler of his adventures, stared at him admiringly.

"I never expected to meet you, er, that is me, face to face," he said.

"Neither did I, Henry," he replied and he noticed that his Dangerfield voice was much deeper than that of the person that was clad in the oversize dinner jacket and wide trousers.

"Are you taking her with you?"

"It won't be necessary," he replied. "Just give me the money."

"Such," said the voice of the late P. W. Arnold, "was the command in the tone of Dangerfield's voice that the small pale-faced author went immediately to his bed. The very bed," added the Voice, "that the famous madcap explorer and adventurer and writer breathed his last in. Much to the regret," it added, "of some of the most beautiful women in the world, and produced from under the mattress a bundle of notes."

"How much do you want?" said Mr Potts.

"All of it," he replied, and seeing the reluctant look, he added, "you do want to get rid of her, don't you?"

Pocketing the money he ran lightly down the stairs and stopped in front of the assembled faces.

"Thank you Mrs Harris," he said, as Elsie handed him his hat.

"Going up to that room was a very special moment for me."

"I quite understand," said Mrs Harris.

"I had been thinking of joining my sister in Wogga Wogga," said Mrs Baldwin grasping his arm.

"Before she got engaged to my friend Mr Potts," said Mr Leopold, giving Mrs Baldwin a stern glance.

Putting on his top hat at a rakish angle, Mr Potts put a hand in his pocket and produced the bundle of notes.

"No time to buy a wedding present," he said apologetically, "but please accept this meagre sum of £600 which I'm sure you can put to good use."

"Oh she couldn't take it," said Mrs Harris.

"Thank you," said Mrs Baldwin.

"Seex hundred pounds," vibrated Signor Baroli, "so much money."

"It'll pay for Sydney's schooling," said Mr Leopold.

Mr Potts couldn't resist it.

"You have a child?" he inquired.

"By a previous husband," said Mrs Baldwin, then hurriedly, "He's very tiny and no trouble."

"He's at Scouts at the moment," said Mr Leopold.

"Cubs," said Mrs Baldwin.

Taking a last look round, Mr Henry Wordsworth Potts bathed himself for the last time in the admiring glances of the occupants of 69 Ranleigh Road and with a flashing smile cried, "Farewell my friends", and pausing as he started for the door, he gazed at Mrs Baldwin and murmured, "If only I hadn't been too late."

"Don't give up, my darling," she whispered.

"I cannot share you with another man," he replied, and despite her restraining hand he headed for the front door which Elsie had opened.

Throwing caution to the wind Mrs Baldwin shouted, "There is no other."

Suddenly the figures in the hall froze. Mr Potts in his role of Dangerfield had a momentary glimpse of the horror-struck face of Mrs Harris, the open mouth of Mr Leopold, the raised admonishing finger of Signor Baroli and the smile of relief on the bespectacled pale face at the foot of the stairs.

His voice broke the silence, "I'm afraid," said Henry Potts the author, "that I must consider the engagement off."

"Quite right," said Signor Baroli and putting an arm round Mrs Baldwin he announced, "I have a tip for a dog running on Saturday, dear Mrs Baldwin, that cannot lose."

They followed in the wake of his lithe, athletic stride to the car. With a quick swing on the handle, the engine started and with a cheery wave and a leap, he was behind the wheel.

"Oh, look at his car," said Mr Leopold, his mouth working excitedly. "Isn't it chic."

"There's a boat on Thursday," shouted Mrs Baldwin desperately, as he engaged the gears.

"Don't be hasty, my darling," said Signor Baroli.

"Signor Baroli," said Mrs Harris, "I hope you will be able to find a room tonight." And putting her arm round the shoulders of the smiling, bespectacled figure she waved goodbye.

"And with an answering wave," said the voice of the late P. W. Arnold, "Dangerfield drove off into the night for his last appointment with the Time Traveller."

The voice died away to be replaced by the clatter of the typewriter keys and above the sound of the keys was a loud knocking. Mr Potts stopped typing.

"Yes," he said. "It's time for you to change," exclaimed Elsie's voice. "I've got your suit what's been altered."

Mr Potts rose in a daze and opened the door. Elsie handed him the suit that the late Mr Harris had passed away in. "Thank you," said Mr Potts dully.

He didn't even bother to close the door. It had seemed so real this time, yet it was just another story, a wishful "what might have been" and at that moment he made up his mind that he was never going to listen to P. W. Arnold again. He'd written his last Dangerfield story. Tomorrow he would dispose of the ancient Imperial. He sat on the bed, in a few hours he'd be officially engaged. P. W. had let him down for the last time.

The front doorbell rang. Probably his stepson Sydney back from his Scout meeting. Married life mustn't be too bad, someone to look after him when he was old.

He heard Elsie's voice call out. "Gent ter see yer, Mrs 'Arris," it screeched. With a bound he flew off the bed and ran to the landing. Hardly daring to breathe, he peered over the bannisters. Standing in the hall was the handsomest man he'd ever seen. For a moment their eyes met. A pained look appeared on the handsomest man's face and he closed his eyes. Mr Potts ran back to his room.

"Yippee!" he shouted. "I'm here!" "Thank you, P. W., thank you." It wasn't the end of the story after all.

His arms suddenly reached out drawn by some invisible force and his fingers leapt to the keys. "No," they typed, "just the beginning."